GOODBYE TO YESTERDAY

Goodbye To Yesterday

by

Sarah Franklin

Dales Large Print Books
Long Preston, North Yorkshire,
BD23 4ND, England.

British Library Cataloguing in Publication Data.

Franklin, Sarah
    Goodbye to yesterday.

    A catalogue record of this book is
    available from the British Library

    ISBN   1-84262-313-3 pbk

First published in Great Britain in 1991 by Mills & Boon Ltd.

Copyright © Sarah Franklin 1991

Cover illustration © John Hancock by arrangement with
P.W.A. International Ltd.

The moral right of the author has been asserted

Published in Large Print 2006 by arrangement with
Jeanne Whitmee, care of Dorian Literary Agency

Dales Large Print is an imprint of Library Magna Books Ltd.

Printed and bound in Great Britain by
T.J. (International) Ltd., Cornwall, PL28 8RW

CHAPTER ONE

In the dimly lit studio on the top floor of St Catherine's Hospital Petra sat at the microphone. Through the glass panel of the control room Toby Bradshaw grinned encouragingly, holding up both his thumbs for good luck. Petra watched for the red light that would tell her she was on the air and listened as Toby faded in the introductory music. She took a deep breath, then began to read the first poem.

The Witching Hour was quite the nicest thing Petra had been asked to do since joining the Radio Cathy team. It had been Toby's idea: a fifteen minute programme of gentle poetry with a background of soothing music, designed for the many insomniacs he had met during his travels around the wards, patients who lay awake into the small hours through pain or worry. Petra had been the inspiration for the programme. With her quiet manner and her beautiful voice he had known right from the first that she would do it beautifully, and he'd been right. From the very first night the programme had gone out the reaction had been more than favourable. Requests poured in – both for favourite poetry and music, but especially asking to know the identity of the girl who presented the programme.

Toby watched through the glass panel as Petra came to the end of the programme, wishing he could think of a way to convince her that she was still beautiful. The facial scars sustained in a fire almost three years ago had changed her whole life, but in Toby's opinion she was wrong to shut herself away from the world as she did. He put on the record that concluded the programme and slipped out into the corridor to the coffee machine, returning just as Petra was switching off her mike.

'It was really great tonight, love.' He handed her one of the plastic cups. 'I don't know where you find those poems, but they're just right.'

'Thanks, Toby.' Petra sipped the hot coffee gratefully. 'I'd better get off home now. Tomorrow is my first day as a fully qualified drama therapist and I want to be up early.'

'I hadn't forgotten.' Toby smiled and pulled a tiny teddy bear key-ring out of his pocket. 'I got you this – for good luck,' he said, holding it up.

Petra's eyes lit up. 'Oh, Toby, how sweet! Thank you.'

'Nervous?'

'No.' She pulled a wry face. 'Well – all right, a bit. Not that I'm not looking forward to it, of course. And it'll be nice to be able to save some money again.'

Toby nodded. He didn't ask what it was she wanted to save for. He wished she'd get the idea out of her head that she needed further plastic surgery, but he knew better than to argue with her about it yet again. Instead he said, 'I know – why don't we meet me in the Crown for lunch tomorrow? Then you can give me an update on how it's all going.'

'Right, that's a date.' She was gathering up her handbag and gloves. 'And now I really must go.' She stood on tiptoe to kiss his cheek. 'See you tomorrow – thanks again for the teddy bear.'

It was a little over two years since Petra had left the security of Maltings Rehabilitation Centre to embark on her training as a drama therapist. A disastrous fire at a friend's firework party three years ago had ended her promising career as an actress and plunged

11

her into months of pain and anguish in the burns unit of St Catherine's, the hospital where she had been working as a part-time clerk while doing her drama therapy training. She had spent most of her free time giving voluntary help with the radio station too, so St Catherine's had become almost a second home to her.

For a long time after she had come out of hospital she had been deeply depressed, unable to come to terms with the facial disfigurement caused by her burns. Even after plastic surgery and skin grafts had eased the tightened muscles on the right side of her face, leaving only the most superficial of scars, the psychological scarring remained. She had been assured again and again that the scars would fade so as to be almost imperceptible. She hadn't believed it – and she still didn't. When she looked into the mirror – something she did as little as she could – all she saw was the end of her hopes and dreams.

It had taken all her courage as well as the help she had received at Maltings to go out into the world on her own again and begin training for a new career. During the past months she had made few friends. Refusing offers and invitations, she had returned to

12

her top-floor flat each evening to study relentlessly, often well into the small hours. All her energy, both physical and emotional, was lavished on the new target she had set herself, determined to put the past with its shattered dream behind her once and for all.

Her only relaxation was the time she spent at Radio Cathy with Toby and his team of cheerful helpers. Here she could be an anonymous voice behind a microphone; here she could do the work she loved, yet still feel safe.

Fortified by the hot coffee, she travelled down in the lift, through the quiet hospital corridors and out to the car park. The sudden chill of the September wind sent fallen leaves swirling around her feet, reminding her that autumn was well and truly here and soon it would be winter. She turned up her coat collar.

As she switched on the car's ignition the thought of tomorrow suddenly hit her, making her stomach muscles tighten. So far, with the help of Toby and her work at Radio Cathy, she had managed to put off thinking about it, but now there was nothing between her and that first day but a night's sleep. Though as she nosed the car on to the road she reflected wryly that she was unlikely to get much sleep tonight. Finally the time had come when she must put her faith in her new abilities and take that first positive step into the future.

In the little rest cubicle on Accident and Emergency, Dr James Ewing took off the headphones and switched off the radio. Whenever he was on duty late at night he liked to listen to *The Witching Hour*. It was one of Toby Bradshaw's better ideas. And the girl who presented it had the most beautiful voice he had ever heard.

Being duty doctor on A and E was either all rush or sheer mind-bending boredom. On quiet nights such as this it was good to have something to listen to other than the endless stream of pop music dished out by the local radio station. He folded his arms behind his head and stretched out his long length on the narrow bed. He really should get some sleep while he could. This lull couldn't possibly last. But as he closed his eyes he found himself wondering – what did she look like, the girl? Her name was Petra, that much he knew. Unusual. Intriguing. Was she blonde? he wondered. No – dark. With a voice like that, so soft and sexy, she

14

just had to be a brunette. He sighed, settling himself more comfortably. She'd be tall, he decided, beginning to build up a picture behind his closed eyelids. Tall and slim, supple as a willow tree. She'd have long dark brown hair and wide, expressive brown – no, the eyes would be a fascinating grey-green. Her mouth would be soft, generous and sensuous. Eminently kissable. His lips curved into a smile as sleep began to claim him, warm and seductive as a woman's arms. He felt his body beginning to relax – to sink into the bed – then,

'Doctor! Can you come? *Quickly, please!*'

The door of his cubicle was rattled abruptly and the nurse's voice, shrill and strident with urgency, chased away the memory of more dulcet tones. Her head came round the door, white cap perched on top of close-cropped greying hair, spectacles gleaming like laser beams, boring intrudingly into his delicious half-waking dream and bringing him down to reality with a bump.

'Wake up, Dr Ewing! It's an RTA – a nasty pile-up on the motorway. At least six casualties. Ambulances on their way now.'

'All right, Nurse, I'm coming.' He swung his feet to the floor and reached for his stethoscope. Glancing briefly in the mirror, he ran his fingers through his dishevelled hair and dimly registered the stubble darkening his jaw, then, buttoning his white coat as he went, he walked out into the corridor, just in time to meet the first ambulance crew wheeling in the first of the victims.

Petra suspected that her first session, with the children at Queen Matilda's Children's Home, was designed to ease her in gently. Further down her list was a day centre for geriatrics and a special school for disturbed children, each of which offered a different kind of challenge. But the children at Tilly's, as it was affectionately known, promised nothing but delight. Petra had done much of her practical training there and already knew the staff and children well.

When she got out of her car outside the Victorian building the children came running down the steps to welcome her, jostling each other in their haste to get to her. Matron stood smiling in the doorway.

'They've been watching for you since breakfast,' she said. 'Congratulations. Come inside and have a coffee before you begin. I've got the kettle on.'

The children eagerly helped her in with her

boxes of equipment: cassette player and some blank tapes, the collection of percussion instruments and glove puppets she had made with her own hands, and the box of old greetings cards that always came in so useful. The children crowded round as she unpacked, all asking questions at once, eager to know what she had planned for them.

The ninety-minute session flew. They loosened up with some 'fun' exercises, unfolding like flowers, 'blowing each other up' like balloons; they formed into groups and entertained each other with made-up plays, using the glove puppets. After a break they took it in turns to walk through leaves, dance on hot cinders or wade through treacle, with a small prize for the one whose action was guessed the quickest.

When it was time to leave all the children came out to the car, fighting over who should help carry her boxes, vying for her attention. As Petra watched them her heart contracted. Matron and her staff were kind, but these children had no special person of their own. Petra knew only too well how that felt. One small girl especially touched her heart. Six-year-old Jenny had been trapped in the house in which the rest of her family had died. She had suffered burns to

17

her body as well as her face, and she still wore the pressure garments which surgeons hoped would eventually reduce the severity of her scarring. As Petra stowed the last of her boxes into the boot she felt a small hand creep into hers.

'I liked the music and the games, miss.' Jenny's sunny little smile was touchingly lopsided because of the tautness of the skin on one side of her mouth. Shyly she asked, 'Will you come and play with us again, please?'

'Of course I will, Jenny.' Petra bent to touch the soft blonde head. 'I'll be coming to see you every week from now on.'

Petra's next call was at the psychiatric wing of St Catherine's. Patients there who were recovering from severe clinical depression benefited greatly from drama therapy. In this area Petra had so far been an observer and, more recently, an assistant. But from now on she would be in charge. She felt the responsibility keenly. Children were so pliable and easy, so imaginative and responsive. Adults, especially sick ones, were something else entirely, as she knew from her own experience. As she prepared for the session she remembered the occasion at Maltings when

Anna Clare, the occupational therapist, had encouraged her to help by devising some amateur drama therapy. She had chosen the role reversal method, where each took on the role of a fellow patient. That time it had backfired on her quite spectacularly when young Frank Harvey, a paraplegic patient, had chosen to portray Petra herself and had told her some facts about herself that had shocked her deeply. At the time she had been hurt and angry. But once her anger had cooled she had looked at the unpalatable truths and realised how she must appear to others. It had been an important turning point for her.

Unlike the children with their boundless energy, these patients sat in a circle of chairs, some of them slumped, lethargic and bored, neither seeing nor wanting to see. But Petra recognised the attitude of old and was not put off by it. Ignoring their lack of interest, she explained carefully what she wanted them to do – taking on the role of one of their fellow patients and pretending, just for a while, to be them, exchanging their own problems with those of another and thinking of a way to solve them.

At first they were reluctant, but once the first patient had broken the ice the others

19

followed. As the session progressed and 'home truths' began to emerge the bored expressions were gradually replaced by something much more positive. Petra found it fascinating to watch as the whole gamut of emotions from indignation to anxiety, from resentment to downright anger, rippled across the faces of the assembled group. She let them continue, stopping them only when the discussion began to grow heated. Then she lightened the mood by telling them about her own experience with the same method and how it had made her think about herself.

Toby was already waiting when she arrived. The Crown was close to the hospital and very popular with the staff there. It offered good fast bar food, which meant that it was usually crowded, especially on market days. As Petra came in she spotted Toby waving to her from a table near the window, and she noticed that without being asked he had saved her the seat which would place her with her right side away from the room.

'I've ordered for you,' he said as she sat down. 'They've got home-made oxtail soup on the menu, and I know you like that.'

She smiled, slipping her arms out of her coat. 'Thanks, Toby. I don't know when I've felt so hungry. I could eat the whole ox, never mind the tail!'

He watched her as she settled herself, wishing he could break himself of the habit of pandering to her groundless preoccupation over her scars. If he had any sense he would make her sit with her right side towards the room, force her to see that no one noticed the slight tautness that ran from temple to jaw. When she wore the tumbling russet hair loose as she did today it was hidden from view anyway. Even if it weren't, the expressive green eyes and the lovely voice more than made up for it. He sighed. He was prejudiced, of course. Nevertheless, he wished he could convince her.

'What's up – smut on my nose?' She glanced at him enquiringly and he realised he'd been staring at her.

He shook his head. 'No – far from it. You look happier than I've seen you for ages. I take it the morning went well.'

'It did, rather. Mmm...' she sniffed at the fragrant steam rising from the bowl of soup placed in front of her '...this smells good.' She picked up her spoon and applied herself to it. 'Mind you, I'm not kidding myself that it's all going to be as easy as this morning. The kids at Tilly's are sweet and the patients in the psychiatric wing thoroughly enjoyed taking each other apart.' She laughed.

'So what's down for this afternoon?' Toby asked.

Petra reached into her bag for the list. 'Just the one session – with a group of elderly people at the day centre. It's by way of being an experiment. You see, some of them live alone and have forgotten how to communicate. Even though they go to the centre a couple of times a week, they don't speak to anyone, don't get anything out of it. This way we're hoping to get them into the way of talking to each other again.' She put the list back into her bag. 'Then this evening I'll have my reports to write up, of course.'

Toby looked disappointed. 'Oh. I was going to ask you to eat with me. It's my night off Cathy's. I'd like to talk to you about recording a batch of *Witching Hour* programmes. Now that you're working full time it would save you coming in to do it live.'

'That's true.' Petra looked thoughtful. 'Well, maybe I could find time for a quick snack. I'll have to be home early, though.'

'Great!' His face broke into a grin. 'I'll pick you up at seven, shall I? We can have an early meal and then talk for an hour.' He glanced at her tentatively. 'Pet, I've started planning the Christmas shows. I want to do some recording on the wards. How about coming with me?'

The smile left her face and she lowered her eyes. 'You know how I feel about that, Toby.'

He sighed. 'It's so groundless, this worry of yours. Ever since you've been doing the *Witching Hour* programme everyone has been asking to meet you.'

'Better not to disillusion them, then, isn't it?'

Toby shook his head impatiently. 'Honestly, Pet, I don't get it. You're out working with the public now anyway, so what's the difference?'

'I *have* to work,' she told him. 'I have to earn a living. My social life...'

'What did you call it?' he interrupted.

'All right. My *free time* is my own to do as I like with.' The green eyes met his and the message in them was unmistakable. The people she worked with were in the same boat as she was. She felt at home with them.

He gave in. 'All right. But I'm not going to stop asking you...' He broke off, dismayed as she rose and began to put on her coat. 'Oh, look, don't go. I didn't mean to upset you.'

She smiled. 'I'm not upset, Toby. I really

do have to go.' She reached across to touch his hand briefly. 'Thanks for lunch. See you this evening, eh?'

He caught her fingers before she could withdraw them. 'You all right, love?'

'Of course.'

'Sure?'

She gave him the smile that always took his breath away. 'Sure, I'm sure. See you later, Toby.'

He watched her as she made her way through the crowded bar, weaving her way through the tables, tall, elegant, vital. It was such a waste. She was like a modern equivalent of the Sleeping Princess. If only he knew the secret formula that would wake her! Clearly he did not have it.

Toby Bradshaw was a freelance graphics designer. He had come into hospital radio through a friend who was going abroad and wanted someone to take over. Good-natured and naturally gregarious, Toby had taken to the work enthusiastically. Working alone as he did, it was a way of getting out and mixing with people, as well as putting something back into the community, something about which Toby felt strongly. When he had first been introduced to Petra Marshall he hadn't been aware of her scars at all. All he had seen was her lovely face and vibrant personality. She would be both an asset to Radio Cathy and a charming companion. When he had first realised how inhibited she was by the slight scarring on her face he had been appalled.

'People only see *you*,' he told her. 'That dramatic colouring of yours and that voice that could melt concrete at fifty paces. Can't you see? The important part is *you* – what's inside. That's all that really matters, Petra.' But although she always nodded in agreement he knew he hadn't got through to her. Sometimes he despaired of ever getting her back into circulation again.

He got up to leave. The bar was really crowded now and he had to elbow his way through the press of people. As he was passing the bar a voice hailed him.

'Hi, Toby Bradshaw!'

He turned to see Dr James Ewing leaning against the bar, an attractive blonde girl who looked vaguely familiar at his side. He smiled.

'James, hello. Haven't seen you for a while. Where have you been hiding yourself?'

James pulled a face. 'On A and E – all through the night. The graveyard shift, though not nearly as quiet. But it's my day off today, thank goodness. As it happens, I've been enjoying your new brainchild in the quiet moments.'

Toby looked puzzled. 'Brainchild?'

'Yes. *The Witching Hour.*'

Toby grinned. 'Oh, great. It's nice to get some feedback. The patients seem to like it too.'

'I'm not surprised. Er – who did you say the presenter was?'

Toby gave him a wry smile. 'I didn't.'

'Oh, come on, I'm sure you did. The last time I was talking to you, you said she was Petra something or other...' James snapped his fingers. 'Can't quite remember – what was her other name?'

Toby shook his head. 'Nice try, James, but it won't work. I never did tell you her name, and you know it. Anyway, she's far too busy to mix with the likes of you.' Toby glanced at the girl standing at James's side. He recognised her now as a staff nurse on the geriatric ward. He'd seen her there when he recorded a programme a week ago. James Ewing really was the limit! One girl was never enough for him. The Nurses' Home was knee-deep in the hearts he had carelessly broken and tossed aside. Toby was damned sure he wasn't going to subject Petra to cavalier treat-

26

ment of that kind.

'You're wrong, you know,' James insisted. 'I'm sure you gave me her telephone number, but I lost it.'

'If you want to make a request for the programme you can ring the Radio Cathy number.' Toby took in the handsome square jaw with its cleft chin, the dark eyes and thick brown hair. It was nothing short of criminal for one man to have so much going for him. No wonder he was so damned conceited! 'Get your own girls, Ewing,' he said under his breath. 'I've never known you rely on anyone else to get one for you in the past.'

James chuckled. 'Ah, I see what it is now. You're keeping her tucked up your sleeve for a rainy day, are you? Don't you realise that I shall feel positively obliged to take her from you now?'

'It won't be easy,' Toby warned him. 'Petra is her own woman. And anyway, she's dedicated to her career.'

'Which is...?'

'Find out.' Toby shot a glance at the girl at James's side. James interpreted it instantly.

'I'm sorry, I should have introduced you. This is Sandra Hilton. She's on Hayes Ward. She and Gerald Grainger from the Path Lab have just got engaged. We're meeting him

27

here for a drink to celebrate.'

'Oh – I thought...'

James laughed. 'I'm not as insensitive as that! I like my girlfriends one at a time, in spite of what you might have heard. You shouldn't listen to hospital gossip, Toby my lad.'

Toby walked reflectively to his car. Just for once he was grateful for Petra's anti-social tendencies. James Ewing was the last person to help her back into society again. He felt so strongly about it that he decided there and then to do all he could to keep them apart.

CHAPTER TWO

Petra was tired when she got home that evening. She would have been quite happy to have made herself a snack, written up her reports and gone early to bed. But having promised Toby that she would eat with him she felt obliged to keep her promise. Toby had been a good friend to her since she had left Maltings. She felt she owed him a lot.

She was still getting ready when he

arrived. She let him in and asked him to wait while she finished doing her hair. For a moment or two he sat watching as she brushed the heavy auburn mass, then he asked, 'Why don't you pile it all up on top, Petra? It'd suit you.'

She paused to look at him. 'Do I really have to tell you why?'

'But surely with a little skilfully applied make-up...' The moment the words were out he knew he had said the wrong thing.

'No amount of make-up is going to enable me to flaunt my scars like some kind of badge,' she said, colouring warmly. 'So just leave the hairstyle to me, will you, Toby?'

'Of course. I just meant...'

She took his arm. 'Come on, let's go before you say something really silly.'

As they got into his car Toby said, 'I've booked a table at the Waterhole, that new place by the river. Everyone says how good the food is.'

Petra frowned. 'Oh, Toby, I thought we were just going to have a bar snack somewhere.'

He looked crestfallen. 'But it's an occasion, isn't it? Your new job – I thought it deserved more than a pint and a pie.'

She fastened her seat-belt with a snap.

'Toby, you know I hate swish places like that. You might have at least warned me. I could have put on something more dressy.'

He drove in silence. The evening had got off to a bad start. What could he do to make amends?

The Waterhole was the favourite haunt of the fashionable young people of Brentmere, and Petra felt uncomfortable and out of place in her black skirt and white angora sweater. Trust Toby to spring it on her like this! In the cloakroom she took off her coat and ran a comb quickly through her hair, pulling the right side even further forward. She would far rather have gone to the Crown for a snack and then back to the flat to get on with her work. She particularly wanted to turn in good reports this first time, and now they would have to be rushed. Toby clearly wouldn't expect her to eat and run – not at a place like this. She put away the comb and closed her bag with an irritated snap. If *only* he had asked her first!

'Hello. I know you, don't I?'

Petra turned to find herself looking at a pretty blonde girl she vaguely remembered seeing around St Catherine's. 'Hello. Yes, I believe we've met occasionally around the hospital.'

'That's right.' The girl frowned. 'I'm sorry, but I can't quite... You're not on the nursing staff, are you? The hospital is so big that one tends to lose track of who's who.'

'I'm a drama therapist,' Petra told her, surprised at the sudden unexpected thrill of pride the title gave her. 'Petra Marshall. But I'm probably better known for the work I do for Radio Cathy.'

Recognition lit the girl's face. 'Of course, that's it! I remember now. You're doing that new late-night poetry programme, aren't you? I think it's lovely. The older patients love it, and it really does seem to help them off to sleep.'

Petra laughed. 'I'm not sure whether that's a compliment or not, but I know what you mean.'

When she joined Toby in the bar she found that he had ordered her a large gin and tonic and was waiting at a corner table. She looked at him ruefully as she slid into the seat opposite.

'Is this a peace-offering or a mood-sweetener?'

'Neither,' he smiled. 'I just thought you looked tired and it might buck you up.'

'Sorry if I was rotten to you, love.' She picked up the glass and smiled at him over

31

its rim. He was so sweet and thoughtful. He really had meant well, bringing her here. The least she could do was to appear to be enjoying herself.

'Cheers, Toby. Thanks for the thought.'

He raised his own glass and grinned good-naturedly. 'Nice to see you smiling again.'

'Actually I've just had rather a nice compliment,' she told him. 'A nurse from St Cath's was in the powder-room. She was saying how much she liked *The Witching Hour.*'

Toby felt a prickle of unease as he asked, 'Nurse – which one?'

'I don't know. She's from the geriatric wing, I think. She was talking about the older patients, anyway – remarking on how my reading sends them off to sleep. I told her it wasn't...' She stopped speaking, suddenly noticing Toby's expression as he stared over her shoulder. Suddenly he grabbed her arm and said, 'Look, bring your drink in with you. I think our table's ready.'

Before she had time to ask questions she was whisked into the dining-room and seated at a table on the far side of the room.

'I thought we could see everything from here,' Toby explained. Without asking, he had offered her the seat that placed her with her right side against the wall. It was an un-spoken law that neither of them mentioned. The waiter offered them a menu each and Petra studied it, realising as she looked down the list of tempting dishes that she was hungrier than she'd thought.

'The steak Diane looks nice.' She looked up to find Toby staring across the room, his eyes anguished. 'What is it? Have you seen someone you know?' she asked.

Toby was looking across the room to where a party of people were being ushered in. His worst fears were realised as he spotted James Ewing among them – and the girl he'd been with in the Crown at lunchtime. If she knew Petra by sight it would only be a matter of time before she pointed her out to Ewing. And then... Luckily they were seated at a table on the other side of the restaurant, and as he watched he saw to his relief that James Ewing took a seat facing in the other direc-tion.

'Toby, what is it?'

He realised that Petra was speaking to him. 'Oh, it's nothing. Just saw someone I thought I knew.'

'And did you?'

He stared at her. 'Did I what?'

She laughed. 'Really, Toby! Did you see

someone you know?'

'Oh, that. No, I was mistaken.'

Toby was on edge all through the meal, constantly looking over his shoulder to the party on the other side of the room. They seemed to be enjoying themselves – celebrating. He remembered something about the nurse being engaged, to someone in the Path Lab. That must be why they were here. Just so long as Ewing didn't spot them.

Petra ate her steak thoughtfully. Toby was oddly preoccupied. Had she really upset him earlier? It wasn't like him to be moody.

After they had eaten he paid the bill and looked at her.

'Shall we have coffee at my place? I know you don't want to make a late night of it.'

She was surprised. 'It might be better if I make you some at mine. But if I throw you out when you've drunk it, you won't mind will you? I warned you I have my reports to write up, didn't I?'

He nodded in agreement, already getting up from the table. This would be the tricky part; they would have to walk quite close to Ewing's table to get to the door. 'That's fine,' he said abstractedly. 'Of course I don't mind.'

The engagement celebration was in full

34

swing as they passed. Four couples sat round the large table, in the centre of which was an ice bucket holding a bottle of champagne. As Toby hurried past, one hand under Petra's elbow, Sandra Hilton caught sight of them. She waved, but Toby appeared not to notice. On the opposite side of the table James saw the gesture and half turned in his seat.

'Who was that?' he asked.

Sandra shrugged. 'Toby Bradshaw. Funny – I could have sworn he was looking this way, but he didn't see me.'

James watched as the couple disappeared through the glass doors. 'I'm not surprised he doesn't want any intrusions. Who's the gorgeous redhead?'

'That's Petra Marshall,' Sandra told him. 'You know, the girl who does the *Witching Hour* programme. She's the one you were asking Toby about in the pub at lunchtime.'

'*That* was her?' James half rose in his chair, turning towards the door again. But they had gone. He resumed his seat with a wry grin. 'Well, no wonder he's keeping her under wraps!' He turned to Sandra again. 'You don't happen to know her telephone number, I suppose?'

She laughed. 'No. But I imagine she must be in the book.' She leaned across to whisper in his ear, 'James, in case you've forgotten, your date for the evening is sitting on your other side. At this moment she's looking rather miffed. Isn't it time you paid her some attention?'

At the flat Petra made coffee, and Toby drank it thoughtfully. She looked at him.

'Toby, is anything the matter?'

He looked up. 'No – why?'

'You suddenly became – I don't know – preoccupied, back there at the restaurant.'

He forced a laugh. 'I'm fine, really. It's just that I've been thinking – *The Witching Hour* has been so successful, I think it's time we put it out every night instead of just a couple of times a week. I know you're busy, but could you look out some material and plan some programmes in advance? Maybe we could do some recording at the weekend.'

'All right.' She frowned. 'It might be difficult to find enough of the right kind of poems. Could you ask patients to send in some more requests?'

'Sure – good idea. I'll do that.'

'Who did you see at the restaurant, Toby?' Petra added.

He avoided her eyes. 'Oh, just a group from the hospital, some of the more flippant

36

types. I didn't want us to have to share the evening with them.'

For a moment she was silent, then, 'Toby, you're not embarrassed to be seen with me, are you?'

He looked up, startled by her direct question. '*Petra*, of course I'm not! Good God, it's quite the reverse. Whatever makes you ask a question like that?'

She shrugged, getting up to pour more coffee. 'You've always been so kind. You've helped me so much since I left Maltings. I'm grateful, you know that. But I wouldn't want you to feel – well, responsible for me.'

Toby was on his feet. 'For heaven's sake, Petra, what brought this on? It's true that I worry about your relying too much on me. But only because I feel you should be enjoying your life more – getting out and making friends, meeting people.'

'Is that why you didn't want to introduce me to your friends this evening?'

'*No!* That was for a completely different reason.'

'Which was...?'

Trapped, Toby spluttered a little. 'When I said you should meet people, I meant it, of course. But there are certain types I wouldn't expose you to.'

'Really? Why is that?'

He shrugged, acutely uncomfortable. 'Some people are brash and – and tactless. I wouldn't want you to meet the wrong kind of people.'

Petra shook her head at him. 'And you say you aren't over-protective!'

'Maybe I just want to keep you to myself, Petra,' he said softly.

'And maybe you're resorting to flattery to get off the hook.' She laughed at his crestfallen expression and looked at her watch. 'Sorry, Toby, that wasn't fair. Anyway, it's high time I threw you out and did some work.'

He stood up. 'Of course – thoughtless of me. You have your reports to write.'

At the door she put her hand on his shoulder and kissed his cheek. 'Thanks for a lovely evening, Toby. It was a super meal.' She looked at him closely. 'Can I say something?'

'Of course.' His heart sank. He had a pretty good idea what she was about to say.

'I can take care of myself, Toby, honestly. I'll integrate back into society eventually, but I'll have to do it in my own time and my own way. I'm grateful for all your help. But don't try to shield me too much, eh?'

He gave her a wry smile. 'Are you telling

me to get lost? Am I being too possessive?'

'I'm telling you that I can – just about – keep my head above water now. I'm asking you to give me the chance to try a few strokes alone.'

When Toby had gone Petra sat for a long time, deep in thought. Toby was a dear, but was he getting a little too fond of her? She hoped not. It would spoil what, till now, had been a happy, relaxed friendship. A long time ago, even before her accident, she had told herself that her career was all she wanted. There would be no man in her life. Her future was too important to put into the hands of a member of the opposite sex. For a brief while there had been Charles Bennett, of course. He had almost changed her mind and for a few brief months they had been engaged. When he had come back into her life while she had been at Maltings, offering love when she was at her most vulnerable, promising to help her resume her career as an actress just when she thought it was over, she had almost changed her mind. But his cruel betrayal and its shattering effect on her new-found confidence had proved to her that her first instincts had been right. Now she knew for certain that never again could she trust that treacherous emotion called love. The price was far too high. Toby had never been – could never *be* more than a caring friend.

She took a bath, then settled down in her dressing-gown to write the reports. She had almost finished when the telephone rang. The sound startled her, especially when she glanced at her watch and saw that it was almost midnight. Then, deciding that it was probably Toby, she lifted the receiver.

'Hello, Petra Marshall speaking.'

'Hello. I hope you'll forgive me for ringing at this late hour.' The voice was deep, male and attractive. Petra was instantly on her guard.

'Who am I speaking to?' she asked cautiously.

'Ah! You don't know me, but I'm a fan of your programme, *The Witching Hour*. I work at St Catherine's too, you see, and I do know you – well, by sight.'

'Do you also have a name?'

'Of course – I'm sorry. James Ewing – Dr James Ewing.'

'Is there some way in which I can help you, Dr Ewing?' Petra asked. 'Only it is rather late and...'

'I know. And this is quite unforgivable of

me. I just wondered if we might meet some time. You see, I already know you in a way, and I feel sure we have a lot in common.'

Petra felt her hackles rise. 'Is this some kind of a joke?'

'Oh, *no*, I assure you... Please don't hang up, Petra. I can call you Petra, can't I?'

'Look, Dr Ewing – if that's really who you are – could you please just tell me what it is you want, then we can both get some rest?' She found that the hand that held the receiver was shaking. He didn't *sound* like a heavy breather, but what normal person rang a complete stranger at this hour of the night?

'Look, I know this must sound like some kind of line, but I've listened to your programme a lot lately. I've been on duty in A and E, you see. You must be aware that you have a beautiful voice, and I'd like very much indeed to meet you.'

'I'm sorry, Dr Ewing, but I'm afraid that won't be possible,' she told him coolly. 'I don't go on blind dates. In fact, I don't go on dates at all.'

'Ah, now I don't think that's quite true. I happen to know that you were on one tonight.'

A small astonished gasp escaped her. She could hardly believe what she was hearing.

41

'Goodnight, Dr Ewing,' she said icily, firmly replacing the receiver. Whoever he was, he had a king-sized nerve, and probably an ego to match. What had he expected – that she'd agree to go out with him on the strength of such a call, without having so much as set eyes on him? He must be one of two things: either atrociously conceited or completely mad. Either way she wanted nothing to do with him.

Later, as she prepared for bed, she caught sight of herself in the dressing-table mirror. He must have been lying when he'd said he knew her by sight. If he'd ever seen her he certainly wouldn't have been ringing to ask her for a date. Slowly and deliberately she lifted the hair away from the right side of her face and turned her head, forcing herself to take a long, hard look. Once she'd had beauty. Yes, she could say it now – now that it had gone for ever. Surgery had helped. It was better than it had been at first, she admitted that. But nothing could ever restore the flawless skin and the pure contours she had once been so proud of. And if Dr James Ewing had ever *really* seen her he certainly wouldn't have made that call this evening.

But long after she'd put out the light, that deep, slightly husky voice echoed on in her

42

mind. In spite of her resentment, she found herself wondering if he had meant it when he'd said he enjoyed the programme – if he'd been sincere when he said she had a beautiful voice? At least one thing was certain. Unless he had a hide like a rhinoceros he wouldn't be ringing her again.

James lay staring at the square of moonlit sky framed by his bedroom window. Odd – all those endless nights on duty, trying desperately to keep awake and longing for his own bed. Yet now he was in it, with the prospect of a whole night's uninterrupted rest before him, he couldn't seem to fall asleep. He folded his hands behind his head and went over the conversation he had had with Petra Marshall. She had certainly put him in his place. What had he really expected? he asked himself. The glimpse he'd had of her at the restaurant – long legs and tumbling flame-coloured hair, straight nose, beautiful bones and – he thought – flashing green eyes, had led him to expect sophistication, a girl who was used to admiration. He'd imagined that she would exchange a little repartee with him – perhaps she would not agree to see him right away, but would drop some subtle hint, indicating that she might, at some later stage, be willing. Petra's abrupt dismissal was something he had been totally unprepared for. It had surprised and dismayed him. But there were other fish in the sea, he told himself. *Plenty* of other fish. Dr James Ewing had never been short of female company, so why was this particular dismissal so stinging?

He punched his pillow impatiently and turned over. Never in his life had he allowed a woman to spoil his sleep – especially one he'd never even met. And he didn't intend to let this arrogant young woman be the first. An hour later he was still awake. And still telling himself the same thing.

CHAPTER THREE

'Oh, didcup!'

'Don't you speak to me like that. You're a mump! A diggin' old mump!'

The two children faced each other angrily, then the girl caught the boy's hands and began to pull him across the room. He tried to resist, but she was bigger than him and soon he found himself ignominiously sliding, almost in a crouching position, to the other

44

side of the room.

'I *won!*' Sharon shouted triumphantly. 'I beat him – little grit!'

Peter scowled. 'You – you...' He looked at Petra as he searched for a strong enough word. 'You *gunge!*'

The twenty children in the class collapsed with laughter, and the aggression which had hung in the room like a pall of smoke dispersed.

'You see, it can be done,' Petra told them. 'Swear words are only a habit. When you're angry any old word will do to say what you feel. It's only the way you say it.'

The class of children Petra was taking for a drama therapy class attended a special school. They were all victims of some kind of abuse, some physical and some mental, and Petra's first task was to try to rid them of their pent-up aggression. She had already had two sessions with the children. The first had been disastrous, when two boys had attacked each other viciously and she had had to get help to part them. But now she began to feel she was getting through to them. She clapped her hands.

'Right, I think that's enough swearing for one day. I think maybe we're ready for a little fencing.'

'Fencing? What's that, miss?'

'Fighting with swords, like they used to in the olden days. Only we won't have real swords, we're just going to pretend them.' She put a hand on the shoulders of the two children nearest to her. 'Now, a sword is about this long...' She extended her hands. 'So as you're both holding one you'll have to stay twice that far apart.' She placed them two swords' distance apart. 'Right, now you've all seen those films on the telly. Off you go!'

Whatever the children lacked, it wasn't imagination. Pair by pair they began to join the two Petra had chosen, to try the mimed fencing. Their enthusiasm grew. There were realistic bloodcurdling yells and cries of, 'Oooh, you've poked me eye out!' and, 'Aaaarh! You got me now – right through the guts!' she even fancied she heard one or two of the made-up swear words used again as harmless lunges were made. But, as she watched, Petra was impressed to find that they were all sticking to the rule of staying two swords' length apart. It really did seem as though she was getting her message across to them. Aggression could be worked out without hurting anyone. They were quite happy to 'attack' even though they weren't even touching their opponents.

Finally she called a halt and the children subsided, panting and exhausted, to the floor, to take a break and drink a mug of milk. While they were resting Petra talked to them about music, trying to discover how much they knew and what they liked. Then she played them a tape. It was a collection of very different kinds of music, ranging from classical to pop. When the empty mugs had been cleared away she invited them to dance.

'Just get up when and if you feel like it,' she told them. 'On your own, in pairs or groups – just however you like. Dance as the music makes you feel.'

At first they just listened, glancing around self-consciously at each other, then, one by one, they stood up and began to express themselves in dance. As Petra had expected, the pop music was the most popular to begin with. The children gyrated, flinging their arms about, swinging their hips and shaking their heads to the beat. When the music suddenly changed to something quieter, they were temporarily thrown. For a moment they stood, listening uncertainly, and one or two sat down again. But slowly the others began to adapt to the music, and Petra was touched to see that some of them showed considerable grace of movement. When the tape came to an end, she asked, 'Did you enjoy that?'

All agreed that they had.

'Would you like us to have a proper dance team?'

They glanced round at each other. Then one boy asked, 'What for, miss?'

'For fun, at first,' she told them. 'But if we turned out to be very good at it, maybe we could put on a show for the rest of the school. Next time I'll bring you a video of some dances from different parts of the world. There are Red Indian dances, Mexican and Spanish – even Scottish reels. We can pick something out and try to learn how to do it. What do you say?'

There were enthusiastic nods of approval all round. At last she'd caught their interest and imagination, and by learning to dance they would be following the discipline that had been sadly lacking in their lives so far.

For the past two weekends Petra had been busy recording *Witching Hour* programmes with Toby. During his record programme he had asked for patients to request a favourite poem, and the response had been over-whelming. Already there were enough poems

48

for several months' programmes, and Petra had been kept busy at the local library, looking them all up and getting them copied. On her way home that afternoon she called in at the hospital to see Toby about arrangements for the weekend. He was not in the studio and Frances, the middle-aged lady who always held the fort for him, told her that he was doing a round of the wards for his Naughtiest Patient of the Week spot. She finally tracked him down on Men's Surgical. For a moment she stood in the doorway, watching as Toby held the microphone of his tape recorder for an elderly man in blue pyjamas as Sister stood by.

'Now then, Mr Pollard, Sister tells me she has great difficulty getting you into the bath. Is this true?'

The old man nodded. 'Only too true, mate. Last time I let a woman come into the bathroom with me I was six years old. I ain't in my second childhood yet.'

'Ah, but you've had an operation, so this is slightly different, isn't it?' Toby asked.

The old man shook his head. 'I'm not undressing in front of any young gel,' he said vehemently. 'If they want to get me in the bath they'll have to get me one o' them there male nurses, I'm not having no slip of a girl watching me take a dip.'

Toby looked at Sister, his eyes twinkling. 'Well, Sister? Does Mr Pollard get his male nurse or does he go without a bath?'

Sister stood at the end of Mr Pollard's bed, eyeing him determinedly. 'Either he lets me help him to the bathroom or he gets a bed-bath,' she said. 'And I mean *this afternoon*. So what's it to be, Mr Pollard?'

Toby turned away and spoke into his mike. 'And so the battle of the bath goes on. Who'll win – Sister or Mr Pollard? I know who my money's on. But I'll leave it to your imagination. What I can tell you is that Mr Bert Pollard wins this week's Naughtiest Patient of the Week Award hands down, and now I'm going to play this record especially for him.' He switched off his mike and turned to Sister. 'I think that should do nicely, thank you, Sister,' he said. 'I'll leave you to struggle with Mr Pollard. And the best of British luck!' He caught sight of Petra and waved. 'Hi. Nice to see you.'

'I've finished for the day and I thought I might still catch the library if you've any more of those requests for me to look up,' she told him.

'There are one or two, but never mind them now.' He took her arm. 'We've plenty of material for the time being. Come up to the canteen and have some tea. Tell me about your day.'

Seated at a corner table with tea and buns, Petra asked, 'Didn't that poor man mind you giving him and his bathing habits all that publicity?'

He laughed. 'Not a bit of it! He lapped it up. Secretly he loves all the attention he gets in hospital. He's been living on his own for the past ten years and he loves having a woman to fuss over him again. I talked to him for quite a while before we started recording.'

'Ah, so it was all set up, was it?'

'Not really. He does make a fuss about his bath, but it's all an act really. He always gives in in the end.'

'So what record will you play for him?'

Toby shrugged. 'I haven't got round to that yet – maybe that old number, "Cool Water".'

She was still laughing when she noticed two white-coated figures coming in. One was a stocky, fair-haired young man; the other was tall and dark, and as he stood in the canteen doorway Petra was struck by his commanding presence. Toby followed the direction of her gaze and said quickly, 'Ah, we can go if you like – if you've finished your tea.'

She looked at him in surprise. 'I haven't finished, actually. Is anything wrong, Toby?'

He coloured. 'No. I just thought...'

'Who's the tall dark man who's just come in?' she asked. But already some instinct deep inside told her the man's identity. Since the night she and Toby had dined at the Waterhole she had received two more calls from Dr James Ewing. On both occasions he had asked to meet her and on both she had refused. But she hadn't hung up on him. He had a way of making her listen to him in spite of herself. She still hadn't worked out quite what it was. His voice? His disarmingly direct manner? Or perhaps it was still a little flattering to be singled out for attention, even though she would never allow herself to respond. The table at which they were seated was on the far side of the room and partly hidden from view by a pillar, so she felt safe in observing the two men.

'Him? Oh, that's Dr James Ewing,' Toby said reluctantly. 'Why do you ask?'

Petra shrugged as she poured more tea. 'I've seen him around, that's all.'

On the other side of the room James drank his tea gratefully. It had been a busy day, but a rather special one. He had just learned that the registrarship he had hoped for, with Mr Bates-Nicholson the plastic surgeon, was to be his. From the beginning of his student days he had dreamed of specialising in plastic surgery, and the chance to work alongside the brilliant John Bates-Nicholson was something that many more experienced doctors would have given their eye-teeth for. He was to start after Christmas, and the anticipation of his new job filled him with excited optimism.

'So you're on your way, then, James?' his friend Paul Fry said wistfully. They had been students together. Paul's ambitions lay in Orthopaedics, but he had been assigned to Mr Graham, the dermatologist, which accounted for his wistfulness.

'Never mind, Paul,' said James. 'You might even find you like dermatology better.' He looked at his friend sympathetically. He really should be showing him more compassion. But at the moment he was thinking that he would have something new to tell Petra next time he rang. His calls to her had become a habit – something he looked forward to. She still hadn't agreed to go out with him, but she hadn't asked him to stop calling either. He had the feeling he was wearing her down. Last time he had even succeeded in making her laugh. That was a distinctly promising sign. So far he had told no one about his telephone calls to her. For James to admit that he was having difficulty in persuading a girl to go out with him was quite unthinkable. His friends would think he was losing his touch. Several times lately he had asked himself why he bothered with a girl who showed so little interest in him. If he really wanted to meet her, all he had to do was to go round to her flat and ring the bell. But somehow he couldn't bring himself to do that. Neither could he stop thinking about her. There was something intriguing about her elusiveness. He found himself looking forward to hearing the sound of her voice – wondering if this time she might just agree to meet him – because he knew that if the decision didn't come from her it would be no good. But these were feelings that none of his friends would understand. The mere idea of James Ewing chasing this ice maiden was ludicrous. So James intended to keep his tenuous and fragile relationship with Petra to himself – at least for a while.

Suddenly he was aware of Paul waving and he looked up to see a trio of nurses coming in. They collected their tea and joined the two housemen, chattering excitedly, eager to hear their news.

Petra averted her eyes as the group of pretty nurses joined James and his friend. Suddenly her heart felt heavy. The girls looked so young and carefree – they obviously hadn't a care in the world. They were not afraid to show *their* faces to the world. They would never have any reason to hide away as she had. Clearly James Ewing, with his good looks and carefree manner, was popular and in demand with the opposite sex. He could have his pick of the adoring young nurses at St Catherine's. He had chosen to pursue *her* on the strength of her voice. If he ever saw her he would soon realise his mistake. Yet why should she care? She hadn't asked him to telephone her. She wished he would stop.

'What's the matter, Petra?' Toby was looking at her oddly.

She dragged her attention away from the group on the other side of the room and forced a laugh. 'Matter? Nothing – why?'

'You were looking so sad and wistful. Has something upset you?'

'No, I'm fine.' She glanced across the room and saw that James was deep in conversation with a vivacious dark-haired girl who was sitting beside him, her head bent close to his.

'Let's go,' she said suddenly. 'The sooner I've been home and freshened up, the sooner we can start on those recordings.'

Somewhat perplexed, Toby followed her as she strode briskly out of the canteen.

In the corridor he caught her arm and swung her round to face him. 'Hang on a minute. Where's the fire?' He looked into her eyes. 'What was it – something I said?'

She shook her head. 'Of course not. I'm sorry, Toby, it isn't you.'

'Then what is it?' When she didn't reply he asked, 'Did you want me to introduce you to that crowd in there? Believe me, Petra, if it had been anyone else, I would. But Ewing isn't your sort. You wouldn't like him.'

'How can you possibly know that?' she asked sharply.

He lifted his shoulders helplessly. 'He's – I don't know – brash and insensitive. You never see him with the same girl twice. You know the kind.'

'I'm not sure that I do. But why should that matter to me, do you suppose?' she asked. 'Or do you think I'd be likely to be bowled over by his charms like some dizzy little teenager? Do I seem that naïve, Toby?'

'Of course not. It's just...'

'I made up my mind long ago that no man

would ever dominate my life, Toby,' she told him. 'Which I think you will agree is a good thing under the circumstances.' She strode ahead of him down the corridor, and after a moment he sighed and followed. Something had caught her on the raw. He only wished he knew what.

By the time Petra got back to her flat that night it was after eleven. They had managed to get a whole week's programmes into the can, as Toby put it, which meant that the weekend was free to spend as she liked. Toby had tentatively suggested that she might go along to the studio and help him edit the material he had recorded on the wards that afternoon, and she had half agreed. Sometimes she felt guilty about Toby. If she weren't around he might find himself a nice girlfriend. He deserved someone who would give him back some of the affection he always gave so generously. Yet whenever she suggested it, Toby told her not to be silly.

She had a leisurely bath and was making herself a hot drink when the telephone rang. She lifted the receiver.

'Hello.'

'Hello, Petra.'

To her surprise and dismay his voice sent

a small frisson of pleasure along her spine. Taking a deep breath, she tried hard to disregard it. 'Oh, it's James. Hello.'

'Clever of you to recognise my voice. How are you?'

'I'm fine – and you?'

'Actually I had some good news today. I'm to be attached to Mr Bates-Nicholson's firm after Christmas.'

'As registrar?'

'That's right. He's a brilliant surgeon. I can hardly believe my luck.'

'I'm glad for you,' said Petra.

'So how about coming out with me to celebrate?'

She bit her lip hard. 'I – can't do that, James. I'm sorry.'

'Oh, come on, you're not still playing hard to get?'

'Not at all. I've told you before, James, it's no use asking me. I'm not going out with you.'

'Just tell me what it is you have against me.'

She sighed. 'I don't have anything against you.'

'Something against men in general, then?'

'That's slightly closer,' she agreed.

'Look, if some idiot jilted you he has to

have been mad. But that's still no reason to...'

'James, it's not like that. Look, I don't want to talk about it.'

He tried another tack. 'Look – if you won't go out with me, will you let me come round and see you?'

Her heart quickened with sudden panic. *'No!* Please, James, it isn't going to work, so please don't ask. There must be dozens of girls all waiting to be asked out by you. Why don't you celebrate your good luck with one of them?'

'Because I happen to want to share it with you. I want to get to know you, Petra. The telephone's no good for that – even you have to admit that.' His voice was soft and seductive, and she swallowed hard. He was a man who was used to getting his own way, she told herself. That was why he was being so persistent. It would do him no harm to be thwarted for once.

'Is it because we've never met?' he asked. 'Because that's easy enough to remedy. I can promise you I'm really quite presentable – or so I'm told.'

'James – look, I'm really glad about your good luck, but I have to go now.'

'Why? Where can you possibly be going at

this time of night?'

'It's late. And I have something on the stove – some milk. It'll boil over.'

'I'll ring again. Petra...' There was a moment's silence, then he asked, 'Do you want me to?'

She opened her mouth to say 'no', but somehow she heard herself saying, 'All right – yes.'

'I warn you, I'm not going to stop asking to meet you.'

'You might as well, James. Because I'm not going out with you. I won't – *can't* change my mind.'

'*Can't?*' He sounded alarmed. 'You're not married – engaged or anything?'

'No.'

'Right, then there's no problem. Goodnight, Petra.'

'Goodnight.' She replaced the receiver and stood staring down at it for a long moment. She'd had the perfect opportunity. Why hadn't she told him not to ring again? Why hadn't she seized the chance he had handed her – lied and said she was already attached? And why didn't she want to know the answers to any of her own questions?

Petra arrived early at Toby's flat. She'd slept

badly and wakened at the crack of dawn. James was beginning to get to her – to make her anxious. She really should be honest with him – tell him the truth about herself. For most of the night she had struggled with the problem. Once he knew that he was asking a woman with a badly scarred face to go out with him he would probably feel foolish and embarrassed. What would his friends think? Petra flushed at the thought. However brash James appeared, she found that she didn't want to be the cause of his discomfort. Next time he rang she must find a way to tell him.

Toby lived in the second-floor flat, one of three in a converted Victorian villa on the edge of the town. In the large north-facing living-room, the corner by the window was given over to his drawing-board and the bench that held his paints, brushes and the other tools of his work. Dressed in paint-spattered jeans and a T-shirt, he greeted her warmly and ushered her in.

'You're just in time for breakfast,' he told her.

She smiled. 'Had it, thanks.'

'Coffee, then? It's freshly made.'

Petra accepted the coffee, wandering across to look at the work on his drawing-board.

'Some illustrations for a children's book,' he told her. 'A commission. It's been great fun to do.'

Petra studied the bright painting on the board with interest. Toby had a brilliant flair for colour. 'This is lovely, Toby. Are there any others?'

'That's the last, as a matter of fact,' he told her. 'The others are in this folder. Have a look if you like.'

She turned the pages, fascinated by the deft brush-work and the brilliance of the drawing. There were ten pictures in all. But the one that Toby pointed out as the book's cover illustration was easily the best. It featured a bonfire. Around it danced children, dressed in brightly coloured scarves and bobble hats, their cheeks rosy and their excited eyes reflecting the flames of the fire. The velvet-black sky was splashed with the stars of an exploding rocket – gold, silver, green and red. In spite of the fact that the picture was filled with joy, Petra struggled to suppress the involuntary shudder that ran through her.

Toby saw her reaction and gently took the folder from her, putting it aside. 'Let me give you some more coffee,' he said, studying her face. She took the refilled mug from him in silence, cupping her hands gratefully around its warmth and looking into the brown steamy liquid.

'It still gets to you, doesn't it?' he said quietly. 'Fire and its associations. Pet, it's time you got it out of your system. You should talk about it. You've tried so hard to overcome the terrible thing that happened to you. I really believed you had. But lately there's been something – I don't know what. Why won't you let me try and help you? Why won't you tell me what's worrying you? Because something is, or my name's not Toby Bradshaw.'

He reached out to touch her arm, but she drew away sharply. Too late she saw the hurt in his eyes and said quickly, 'Oh, Toby, I'm sorry, love. Yes, you're right – there is something, but I have to work it out by myself.' She laughed nervously and got up to wander across the room. 'I wish you didn't know me so well sometimes. You're so perceptive.'

'Is that bad?' he asked quietly.

She shrugged. 'There are some things you don't know about me, Toby. Things that maybe even you wouldn't understand – or like.'

'I doubt that. Try me.'

Petra came back to perch on Toby's work

63

stool. 'A long time ago I told myself I didn't need people,' she began. 'People of either sex. At least, not close to me.'

'Because of your parents?' Toby probed. 'Because of their divorce?'

'In a way. Rely too much on others and they let you down. Oh, not that they always mean to. But you have to stand on your own feet in this world. If you lean too hard on others, who can blame them if they fall down?'

'Fair enough,' Toby nodded. 'But you know the quotation: "No man is an island". We all need each other to some extent. What's more, we need to *need*, Petra.'

She shook her head. 'I wonder if that can be true? You see, the only time I ever allowed myself to need someone – to trust, I was let down; let down just as badly as I could be.'

He raised an eyebrow. 'Want to talk about it?'

She sighed. She wasn't sure whether she should talk about it – even whether she *could* yet. Even though it was nearly two years ago the pain and shame were still deeply and painfully etched on her mind. She looked at Toby's expectant face. 'Well – it was when I was at Maltings,' she began.

'The rehabilitation centre?'

'That's right. You've heard me speak of the occupational therapist there – Anna Clare. She helped me a lot. We became good friends. Then, just when I was beginning to feel I was almost ready to face the world again, someone from my past turned up. He said he'd been abroad and had only just heard about – what had happened to me. He took me out, paid me a lot of attention and didn't even seem to notice my scars. He made me feel like a woman again. Then he began to talk about helping me to make a new start in acting. He said he had a friend who was a television director. One evening he took me to meet him. It was then that the shock came – when I discovered what it was really all about.'

She paused, biting her lip, and Toby prompted, 'What *was* it all about, Petra?'

She raised her eyes to look at him. 'The director friend was about to start making a medical documentary series. He was looking for a burns victim on whom to base one of his programmes.'

'Oh, Petra!'

She shuddered. 'Everything was clear to me then. The very fact that Charles, my friend, had strung me along made it obvious

65

that he knew I'd have refused at once if he'd mentioned it before. It had all been a cleverly worked out plan.'

'What did you do?' asked Toby.

'I'm ashamed to say that I reacted badly. All the confidence I thought I'd built up evaporated. It felt like the end of the world. I just wanted to die.' She paused. 'If it hadn't been for Anna and Dr Stuart, the GP at Saltmere, I might not have been here to tell you about it now.'

He reached out to take her hands. 'But surely you're not going to let that one incident cloud your whole life and all your future relationships, Petra? There are an awful lot of decent people in the world – people capable of caring deeply about you, in spite of what you think now.'

She nodded. 'Maybe. I just prefer to be cautious.'

'So caution is what all this is about?' He squeezed her hands. 'Petra, surely you know me better than that by now. I'd never let you down or hurt you. Surely you can believe that?'

Her eyes widened as she looked at him. He thought she was uncertain of *his* feelings. He thought *he* was the cause of all her anxiety. How could she confide in him about James now?

'Of course, Toby,' she said weakly. 'Of course I believe it.'

CHAPTER FOUR

'Petra?'

'Oh, James!'

'I'm sorry it's so late, but don't hang up on me.'

'I wasn't going to,' said Petra.

'Good. Look, I won't say I understand why you won't go out with me, but I do respect your wishes. It needn't stop us talking now and again, need it?'

Petra let out her breath slowly. At least he wasn't going to try to pin her down this time. 'No, it needn't stop us from talking. Just as long as you don't feel you're wasting your time.'

'That's a strange thing to say! Would I bother to ring at all if I felt I was wasting time?'

'I suppose not,' she admitted.

'Tell me about yourself, Petra.'

'There's nothing much to tell. I'm a drama

therapist. You know about the work I do for Radio Cathy.'

'So – have you been a drama therapist for a long time?'

She smiled in spite of herself. 'Why don't you just ask how old I am?'

He adopted a shocked tone. 'I wouldn't dream of asking anything so ungallant!'

'As a matter of fact, drama therapy wasn't my first choice. I began as an actress.' She winced. What was she saying? At this rate she'd find herself having to explain more than she wanted to. 'And I don't mind anyone knowing my age,' she went on hurriedly. 'I'm twenty-six.'

'And I'm thirty-three. You see, we're making progress.' His smile was obvious, even at the other end of the telephone line.

Thirty-three. Petra's curiosity was aroused. She'd thought he must be younger, only having just completed his pre-reg year at the hospital.

'Medicine wasn't my first choice either, you see,' he explained, as though reading her thoughts. 'I'd done a couple of years teaching before I changed direction.'

'Really? Teaching and medicine are very different,' she said. 'What made you decide to change?'

'A close friend of mine was killed in a car accident,' he told her, his voice suddenly grave. 'I was with him at the time. It was terrible, being so helpless – not knowing what to do. If I'd had even a little knowledge at the time I might have saved his life. At least I'd have been able to make him more comfortable. For months afterwards I couldn't get that thought out of my mind. First I took a course in first aid, but that didn't come anywhere close to satisfying me. I found it all so fascinating, and I soon knew that I wanted to go into it much more deeply. Six months later I'd given up my job in a comprehensive school and started my first year in medical school.'

Petra was impressed. 'That was a big step to take. It took courage.'

'You're right, it did. I'd already qualified, yet here I was, starting all over again, without even knowing whether I had it in me to make it in the medical field. So you see I'm not quite the fly-by-night you took me for.' Before she could protest he said, 'But that's enough about me. What made *you* change direction?'

She took a deep breath, wondering just how much to tell him. 'Well, oddly enough, that was the result of an accident too,' she said. 'I was – injured and – and then ill for a long time afterwards. After seeing so many sick people and the work that others did for them, acting seemed so lightweight and superficial. An occupational therapist friend suggested drama therapy. It seemed like a good idea, so I applied for a grant and took a post-professional course.' It was a slight distortion of the truth, but she told herself that it was justified. And anyway, it was near enough.

'I see. That's interesting.' There was a pause, then James said, 'Petra, the hospital is giving a big bonfire party and fireworks display in aid of one of the children's charities next Tuesday. Will you – be there.'

The word 'fireworks' still turned her stomach to iced water, and she stifled a small gasp. 'No, I shan't be going to that.'

'Oh. Any particular reason?'

'As it happens I have something else planned for that evening.' There was a pause, then she said, 'It's very late. I'll have to go now, James. Goodbye.'

After he had replaced the receiver James sat for some minutes, deep in thought. Somehow he'd done it again. She'd been so much warmer and more relaxed this evening, then suddenly it had happened again – that change of mood; the shutter had come down, cutting off contact between them abruptly. What had he said to make her shy away like that? He hadn't even asked her to go to the fireworks party with him, only if she'd be there. Just when he'd thought he was making some headway, too. He *had* made some headway, though. At least now he knew a little more about her, and she about him, but it was quite clearly going to be a long haul. How his friends would laugh if they ever heard about his fumbling attempts at striking up a relationship with Petra Marshall, the *Witching Hour* girl. He remembered the night she'd been pointed out to him at the Waterhole and wondered what she would say if she knew that he'd seen her. He'd spotted her leaving the hospital canteen the other day too, with Toby Bradshaw. It had only been in the distance, of course, on both occasions. But close enough for him to see that she was as beautiful as her voice promised. Oddly, some instinct warned him not to mention that he had seen her, though he couldn't have said why.

He wondered about the accident she had mentioned, and if it had anything to do with her reluctance to take their relationship further. Perhaps she had lost someone she'd cared for very deeply. She couldn't know that he'd lost someone too. She couldn't know about Sarah, to whom he'd been engaged when he'd decided to leave teaching and study medicine – Sarah, whose patience ran out as quickly as her love. The thought that Petra might have something of the kind in common with him intrigued him. He was learning things about himself lately; discovering facets of his character that constantly surprised him. It was a sobering experience.

Petra looked at her watch. It was almost midnight again. James's calls seemed to have fallen into a pattern; he seemed to ring either very early in the evening or very late. 'He must fit me in among all his pressing social arrangements,' she said tartly to herself, then pulled herself up sharply. He had every right to do as he liked with his free time, just as she had. She wondered what he would say if he knew she had seen him in the hospital canteen the other day. And at the restaurant with Toby. For a moment she allowed herself to visualise him: tall, with dark, laughing eyes and a debonair manner. He looked as though life hadn't touched him at all – yet he'd experienced the loss of a close friend. Perhaps there was more to him than she'd imagined after all.

James's call was the second she'd had that Sunday evening. The first had been from Anna. Since Petra had left Maltings they had kept in touch. Married now to Dr Ewan Stuart, Anna still worked as an occupational therapist at the rehabilitation centre. Tonight she had been bubbling over with excitement.

'Guess what, Petra? I'm pregnant. Ewan and I are expecting our first baby!'

'Anna, how lovely! When?'

'Oh, not for ages yet. Next May.'

'Congratulations. Is Ewan pleased?'

'Delighted. We wondered if you'd care to come over to dinner next Tuesday, by way of a little celebration. Bring Toby too, of course. We'd love to meet him.'

'I'd love to come, Anna.' Petra paused. 'But I won't bring Toby this time, if you don't mind. As a matter of fact, I'd appreciate a little chat and some advice.'

'I see. Nothing wrong, I hope?' Anna's tone was concerned.

'No, not wrong exactly. Just difficult.'

'Well, you know I'll help in any way I can, love. Pity about Toby, though. He would have made the number even.'

'Oh, it's a dinner party, is it? I don't know...'

'No, it's *not* a dinner party. Stop panicking! I'm only asking you. It's just that it would be nice for Ewan to have another man to talk to while we're having this heart-to-heart. Petra, you're not still shy about meeting people, are you?'

'No, of course I'm not. It's just – well, you know.'

'Mmm, I'm afraid I do. Sounds as though that talk you mentioned is overdue. I'll look forward to seeing you on Tuesday, then – about seven.'

'Great. I'll be there.'

When James had asked her to go to the fireworks party at the hospital she'd been glad she had a valid reason to refuse. Even if the thought of fireworks hadn't made her blood run cold she wouldn't have been able to go. She was glad. There were enough half-truths in her life.

The moment Petra arrived at Tilly's on Monday morning she realised that something was wrong. There were no eager children waiting for her on the steps and instead of the usual bustling vitality, there was an ominous hush about the place. She soon discovered why. She was unpacking the car when Sharon Griggs, the housekeeper, came out to her.

'Oh, Miss Marshall, I'm so glad to see you! Something dreadful has happened and the children are so upset. Maybe your class will help take their mind off things.'

'Why, what's happened?' Petra asked.

'It's little Jenny Brown. She was knocked down by a car when the children were out for a walk yesterday afternoon.'

'Jenny? Oh, no, not Jenny!' Petra was shocked. Hadn't the poor child suffered enough already? 'Was she badly hurt?'

'Badly enough. A head injury. She's in intensive care at St Catherine's.'

Matron had joined them. She looked tired and worn through lack of sleep. 'I expect you've heard our sad news,' she said. 'The children are badly in need of something to cheer them up this morning. Some of them saw it happen.'

'How awful!' Petra unloaded the last of her boxes and closed the boot. 'Is there anyone who can visit Jenny? Any relatives at all?'

Matron shook her head. 'As you know, she lost both parents in the fire and there are no other relatives at all.'

'I'll go and see her,' said Petra. 'I'll go this evening when I've finished work.'

'She's still unconscious,' Matron said. 'The consultant can't be sure yet how much damage has been done.' She turned away, walking up the steps with drooping shoulders. Sharon shook her head.

'She was at the hospital most of last night. She blames herself, I'm afraid,' she said quietly. 'Though it wasn't her fault. The car was out of control, and it mounted the pavement. There was nothing anyone could have done. It's only surprising that more of the children weren't hurt.'

Although Petra did her best to keep the children occupied there was an air of restlessness about them. When it came to making up plays with the glove puppets, one group decided to stage an accident in which a child was knocked down by a car. Recognising their need to act out their anxiety, Petra encouraged them.

'Is this Jenny?' she asked, picking up the limp puppet. 'What do you think will happen now?' She looked around at the group of small upturned faces.

'Hospital,' said one little boy. 'The ambulance came and took Jenny to the hospital.'

'And what do you think will happen there?'

The children looked at each other.

76

'Mrs Phillips, the cleaning lady, went to hospital. She got a baby there,' one little girl said optimistically.

'Only *ladies* have babies, silly,' the boy told her scathingly. 'Jenny got run over. She'll probably die.'

Two of the more timid children began to cry, and Petra admonished the boy.

'Of course Jenny won't die, Derek! They'll make her better again at the hospital. That's what hospitals are for.'

'The hospital didn't make my mum better,' said a sad little voice from the back. 'That's why I had to come and live here. They don't always make people better. They didn't make Jenny's mum and dad better either, did they?'

Petra swallowed hard. These children had learned the harsh realities of life earlier than most. There was no deceiving them. Maybe it was wrong even to try.

'I promise you that they'll try their hardest to make Jenny better,' she told them. 'They always try the very best they can. And we must all hope as hard as we can for Jenny, and remember to say a little prayer for her too. I'm going to see her this evening. I'll give her your love, shall I? And I'll tell her that you're all thinking about her.' She opened her box of dressing-up clothes, looking for something to divert them. 'Now, to finish up, how about some music and dressing-up? I know you all love to dance.'

Petra's last session of the day was at St Catherine's at the psychiatric wing. As soon as she had finished she went up to Intensive Care and asked if she might see Jenny.

'Just for a minute, though she's still unconscious.' Sister looked at her. 'You're not a relative, are you?'

'She has no relatives,' Petra said. 'Her parents were both killed. I take the children at Queen Matilda's Children's Home, where Jenny lives, for drama therapy. I heard about her accident this morning and I said I'd look in.'

'Poor little scrap,' Sister said, shaking her head. 'She didn't deserve this.'

Petra followed her along the hushed aisle between the cubicles each with its own monitor and array of life-saving technology. Here in the intensive care unit there was no sound, except for the bleeping of the monitors. All the patients were either unconscious or heavily sedated. It was a timeless, seasonless place where day and night merged and life seemed suspended. Petra felt a chill run through her in spite of the steady temperature.

Jenny lay motionless in the bed, her little face paper-white and her eyes closed. Her breathing was assisted by a ventilator. Petra looked down with dismay at the wires and tubes connected to the tiny body.

'As she's unable to take nourishment, she's being fed through a gastric tube,' Sister explained, seeing Petra's expression. 'And the electrodes attached to her chest are to monitor her heartbeat. Her temperature and pulse are taken and recorded every fifteen minutes.' Sister smiled reassuringly. 'It might look like something from a science fiction movie, but it's all necessary for her recovery, I assure you.'

'Oh, I'm sure it is,' Petra said hurriedly. 'It's just – she looks so little and...'

'Defenceless?' Sister supplied. 'I know, my dear. But she's quite a strong little thing, and she's holding her own.'

'She will be all right, won't she? The Matron at Queen Matilda's said something about a danger of brain damage.'

'Until the haematoma reduces we shan't really know the extent of any damage that may have been done,' Sister explained. 'There may be none at all. The blow she received caused bleeding inside the skull, you see, so because of that X-rays are of little use at the moment. We have to wait until the swelling goes down.'

Petra sat beside the bed for a while. Never in her life had she felt so helpless. James's words came back to her. She knew how he must have felt when his friend was fatally injured. But at least everything was being done for Jenny.

Although Jenny was unconscious, she talked to her. She had read somewhere that sometimes unconscious patients could register sounds and sometimes even respond to them. But although she called the child by name, told her what her friends at Tilly's had been doing and the messages they had sent, there was no response, no glimmer of life; not even an involuntary muscle spasm. Petra remembered the time when she herself had lain in hospital after the fire. The pain of her burns had been hard to bear. But having no one to care about her, to hold her hand lovingly and help her through the worst, had been infinitely worse. The memory was harrowing, and tears pricked her eyes. Someone had to be there for Jenny – even though she couldn't hear.

'I'm sorry, Miss Marshall, but I'm afraid I shall have to ask you to leave.' Sister had returned with her staff nurse. 'We have to do

Jenny's fifteen-minute checks now. You can come again tomorrow if you like.'

As Petra walked out to the car park it was beginning to rain. As the icy needles stung her face she made a solemn promise. Jenny should not lie there alone day after day as she had done. She'd visit every day, even though Jenny was unconscious. And afterwards, when she regained consciousness, for as long as the child needed her.

On Tuesday evening Petra was a little late arriving at Anna's. She explained to her hosts that she had been to visit Jenny first.

'She still hasn't regained consciousness, although Sister tells me that X-rays have been done now. So far there's no sign of brain damage, thank goodness.' She took off her coat and handed it to Anna. 'She's breathing unaided now, and her level of unconsciousness is lighter than it was,' she went on. 'Sister seems to think that I might soon get some response if I persevere. While I was driving over I had this idea. Suppose I record some messages from the other children at Tilly's; some of Jenny's favourite music too, and play the tape to her next time I go?'

Ewan nodded approvingly. 'That kind of thing has been most successful in the past.

81

It's certainly worth a try.'

Anna and Ewan lived in a delightfully re-stored cottage in Hazelbridge where Ewan's practice was. They had bought it almost a year ago and had recently moved in after the extensive restoration work had been carried out. It was the first time Petra had seen it, and Anna showed her round proudly. In the living-room a log fire crackled and blazed in the stone fireplace. Petra looked around her appreciatively.

'You've made it so lovely,' she remarked. 'Who would recognise it from the tumble-down wreck you bought?'

'And just in time for the baby,' Ewan said with a smile, handing her a glass of sherry. 'That was all we needed to make everything perfect.' He slipped an arm round Anna's shoulders, and Petra stifled the twinge of envy she felt at the radiant happiness on both their faces as they looked at each other. Ewan and Anna had had their share of troubles, but it seemed that they had everything they could possibly want now.

'I haven't congratulated you both yet,' she said, holding up her glass. 'Here's to the latest addition to the Stuart family. What do you want – boy or girl?'

Ewan laughed. 'Maybe we'll be extra lucky

and get one of each.'

Anna shot him a look. 'Speak for yourself! One at a time will be fine as far as I'm concerned,' she laughed. 'Bring your drink and come into the kitchen with me, Petra, while I put the finishing touches to the meal,' she said.

'You girls!' chuckled Ewan, pouring himself another drink. 'Who do you think you're kidding? Why don't you just say, "Let's leave him in here while we go and have a good gossip"?'

The kitchen had been built on at the rear of the cottage and was equipped with every convenience. Petra thought of the curtained-off corner of her tiny flat, comparing it unfavourably with the elegance of Anna's natural pine units and wipe-clean worktops.

'It's lovely, Anna,' she remarked. 'You have so much space.' She perched on one of the stools at the breakfast bar. 'This makes my so-called flat look like a hovel!'

'Surely you'll soon be able to afford something better?' Anna said, opening the oven to check the roast. 'Maybe you could even go shares with a couple of friends and buy a house.' She glanced round at Petra. 'You have *made* friends, haven't you?'

Petra shrugged noncommittally. 'There

hasn't been a lot of time for socialising. There's still only Toby – except...'

Anna hung up her oven gloves and turned to look at her friend with interest. 'You've fallen out?'

Petra shook her head. 'No, nothing like that.'

'Ah, it's not to do with Toby, then. Do I detect something in the air? Have you met someone – a man?'

Petra shook her head firmly. 'You should know better than to ask me that, Anna. After what happened with Charles I...'

'Oh, *stuff* Charles,' Anna said bluntly. 'That's all in the past. There are plenty of nice decent men around. Charles was just unfortunate.' She peered at Petra. 'So if it isn't a man, who is it?'

'Well, it *is* a man, though I haven't actually met him.'

Anna pulled a face. 'So how do you communicate – thought transference?'

'Telephone, actually.'

'Mmm – intriguing. Go on.'

'Well, you know I've been doing this late-night music and poetry programme on Radio Cathy for Toby?' Petra said.

'Don't tell me – you've had some fan mail?'

'In a way.'

Anna frowned. 'I'd be careful of forming friendships with total strangers if I were you. Surely if he were on the level he'd have asked to meet you by now?'

'He isn't a total stranger, he's a doctor at St Cath's. I've even seen him – in the distance. And he *has* asked to meet me.'

'And you've refused.' Anna sighed. 'Oh, Petra, *why?*'

Petra shook her head. 'Don't you see? He's only heard my voice. Can you imagine what he'd feel when he saw me? It would be too embarrassing to contemplate.'

Anna turned to look at her. Petra was wearing a soft wool dress in a subtle shade of sea-green that accentuated her slim figure and complemented her colouring dramatically. Her hair was caught back on the left side in the way she always wore it, to fall forward, concealing the scarred side of her face.

'Isn't it time you had a change of hairstyle?' Anna asked briskly. She turned Petra round to face a small mirror that hung by the door. Then she drew back the hair on the right side of her face and taking a hairpin from her own hair, secured it firmly. 'There, that's better. It shows off those high cheekbones. Your face is a lovely shape, Petra. It's a shame to hide it.'

Petra shuddered and turned away. 'Don't! You know I can't bear it to be visible like that.'

'But it's improved so much. There's hardly anything to see now,' Anna said reprovingly. 'Honestly, Petra, you have so much – yes, you *do*. There are people around who haven't one iota of the looks you have and still manage to feel confident enough to enjoy life.' She shook her head exasperatedly. 'You know, sometimes I think you cling to those scars; make them an excuse for opting out.'

'That's not fair! You of all people should know how hard I've tried.'

Immediately regretting her hasty words, Anna threw her arms around Petra and hugged her. 'Of course I know, love. I didn't mean to upset you. It's just that I want you to be happy, and seeing you hiding yourself away like this is so frustrating. Let's change the subject. Tell me about your work.'

Their argument temporarily put aside, Petra launched into an enthusiastic account of her work, while Anna busied herself with the vegetables. She had just taken a bottle of wine from the rack and reached for the corkscrew when the doorbell rang. She looked up.

'Oh, Ewan will get that,' she said with a glance at Petra. 'Er – actually, he asked a colleague to drop in. He didn't think he'd be free, but it seems he's made it after all.' She took a dish of vegetables from the oven and handed it to Petra. 'Take that into the dining-room for me, will you, love? The trolley is switched on.' She looked around. 'Right, I think we're about ready to eat now. If you wouldn't mind popping your head round the door and telling them it's ready...'

'You said it would only be me,' Petra said accusingly. Although she would not have admitted it, her heart was drumming in the sickening way it always did when she had to confront a stranger. Hurriedly she put down the dish she was holding and unpinned the hair that Anna had caught back.

Anna shook her head. 'I thought it would – honestly. Ewan didn't tell me until this evening. You look fine, Petra. I wish you'd believe me. You don't have a thing to worry about.'

'It seems I have no choice but to go along with it now, doesn't it? But I do wish you'd told me – given me some warning,' Petra said unhappily.

'So that you could think up an excuse to leave?' Anna laid a hand on her arm. 'Look, Petra, it really *is* time you were made to see what you're missing. I just want you to see how pleasant it can be to meet new people.'

'Why does everyone want to run my life for me?' Petra picked up the dish of vegetables. 'Why can't you all just leave me alone?'

Anna sighed as she watched her go. It was true that Petra had made great strides in training and qualifying for her new career. But when it came to making a new personal life she was much the same as she had been at Maltings two years ago. If only she could meet a man who would give her back her confidence again!

Petra carried her dish of vegetables through to the dining-room and put it into the heated trolley. Across the hall the buzz of male voices came from behind the living-room door. Standing outside, she paused, hating herself for the uncontrollable pounding of her heart. Why should she have to tolerate this? she asked herself. Why didn't she just get her coat and leave now? That would be chickening out, a small voice told her mockingly. She swallowed hard and opened the door defiantly.

'Anna asked me to tell you that dinner is...' She stopped in mid-sentence as a tall dark man rose from the settee where he had been sitting, his back towards her. His eyes were as startled as hers as they met. Ewan got to his feet.

'Oh, Petra, I'd like you to meet my friend James Ewing. James, this is Petra Marshall.'

James held out his hand, his startled look dissolving into a smile. 'So–' he said '–we meet at last, Petra.'

CHAPTER FIVE

Petra froze. The hand she gave to James was cold as ice. Then, as he took it in his warm grip and held it, she felt a warm flush creep painfully and slowly up her neck to stain her cheeks with colour.

Hating herself, James and her host and hostess, she said coolly, 'How do you do?'

Ewan was looking from one to the other curiously. 'You two know each other?' He spoke as though he hadn't quite worked it out.

James shook his head. 'Not exactly. Petra's been doing a late-night programme of poetry for the hospital radio, and I'm her biggest fan. We've spoken on the telephone once or twice.'

His voice was cool and controlled, and the rapid beating of Petra's heart began to slow. Anna looked in.

'Ewan, will you come and uncork the wine? I can never manage to work that trendy corkscrew thing you bought.'

'OK – coming,' Ewan laughed. 'Excuse me, will you? Go through to the dining-room. We'll be with you in a minute.'

When he had gone James looked at Petra. She averted her head and said, 'Shall we go through?'

'In a minute. It's good to meet you at last, Petra.'

'I – had no idea you'd be here this evening,' she said, edging towards the door.

'That sounds as though you wouldn't have come if you'd known.'

'No, I didn't mean that. It was just...'

'A shock?' He smiled at her.

She smiled back in spite of herself. 'I was going to say a surprise.'

'Ah, yes, that does sound nicer.' He reached out and took her hand. 'Shall we go through as they said?'

Petra found herself beginning to relax. If he had noticed her scar he hadn't shown it. He was obviously far too polite. Anyway, with her hair in this style it wasn't too noticeable.

At Anna's round dining-table Petra made sure she sat on James's right-hand side. The meal was delicious, and Anna and Ewan made sure that the conversation didn't lag. Petra was encouraged to talk about her work. And she found that when she did, she lost her shyness and was able to relax even more. She told them about the way the elderly people at the day centre were responding to her sessions and learning how to communicate with each other again. And she related some of the amusing incidents she had encountered with the children at the Bridgemount special school, especially their substitute 'swear words'. The meal over, they moved into the lounge for coffee and talked on. But Petra became a little uneasy when Anna began reminiscing about their time together at Maltings and passing on news of past patients whom Petra knew.

'You worked at Maltings too, then?' James said at last. 'I was wondering how you came to meet these two characters.'

'No, I was a patient there.' Petra's tone was firm. 'I believe I told you about the – accident I was involved in. I completed my recovery at Maltings.'

There was a brief, uneasy silence, then James said quickly, 'Well, you couldn't have been in better hands.'

'You're right there. I owe Anna and Ewan a great deal.' She looked at her watch and got to her feet. 'Heavens, I'd no idea it was so late! I'll have to be going.'

Anna fetched her coat and she thanked them both for her evening, then James said, 'Petra, I hate to ask, but I suppose you couldn't give me a lift, could you? My car's in for servicing at the moment. I came here by taxi.'

She was slightly taken aback, but it would have looked churlish to refuse, so she said, 'Oh – well, yes, of course, if you're ready to go now.'

In the hall Anna managed to whisper, 'I didn't say too much, did I?'

Petra shook her head. 'No. You're right, it's time I stopped trying to sweep things under the carpet.'

Anna looked at her enquiringly. 'Petra, is James the one you were telling me about – the man who's been ringing you?'

'How did you guess?'

'When Ewan came out into the kitchen he told me James had mentioned that you'd spoken once or twice on the phone. I put two and two together.'

'I see.' Petra buttoned her coat. 'I must

confess I'd wondered if it was all a put-up job. He told me he was helping at the hospital fireworks party this evening.'

'No, it was sheer coincidence, I promise you. It seems he put in his stint at the party before he arrived here. That's why he was late.' Anna grinned. 'Though it couldn't have been a happier coincidence as far as I'm concerned. He *is* rather nice, isn't he?'

Petra gave a non-committal little shrug. 'He's all right, I suppose.' She gave Anna a quick hug. 'Thanks for a lovely evening. I'll be in touch. Goodnight.'

In the car as James fastened his seatbelt, she asked, 'Where can I drop you?'

'Hamlyn Street. I share a house with two other housemen.' He looked at her. 'Is that out of your way?'

'No, in fact it's only...' She had been about to say, 'Just round the corner,' but she stopped herself just in time. He sensed her reticence.

'I was rather hoping you might invite me for a nightcap,' he said, his eyes twinkling. 'After all, we're quite close neighbours, aren't we?'

'Yes, I suppose we are.' She felt herself colouring. Of course, he must have seen her address in the telephone book. 'No, no nightcap,' she told him firmly, her eyes on the road ahead.

'Ah, pity. Maybe some other time, when you know me better.' After a pause he said, 'Look, you won't do that without us making some kind of effort, will you, so now that you've seen that I don't have two heads or horns or anything, perhaps we can arrange to meet again. Dinner perhaps...?'

She sat for a moment, silently looking down at her hands, then she said, 'James, you mustn't feel you have to ask me. It's perfectly all right. I shan't think...'

'What are you talking about?' He reached out to cup her chin and turn her face towards him. As he did so, her hair caught against the collar of her coat, pulling it back to expose the scarred side of her face. Angrily she dashed his hand away and turned away again.

'Don't!' she exclaimed.

Silently he took both her hands and held them firmly in his, peering at her intently. After a moment he said, 'Is that what happened, Petra? Your accident – is this why you've been hiding from me?'

She felt her throat thicken and realised with horror that she was perilously close to tears. 'Please – I don't want to talk about it.'

'Of course not,' he said gently. 'But look at me, Petra.'

She raised her head, steeling herself to turn until her eyes met his. Very gently he lifted her hair and held it back, touching the scar tissue with his fingertips.

'So this is the reason you wouldn't see me. But it's barely noticeable, it's so insignificant. It would be terrible to let it spoil your life.'

'I *don't*,' she said defensively. 'I have a very good life. I have my job, my hobby and...'

'Friends?' he put in. 'Oh, I know you have Anna and Ewan, but if you've been around for all this time, why haven't I seen you mixing socially before?'

'I do have friends,' she said quickly. 'Toby, for one – Toby Bradshaw.'

'Ah, yes, Toby,' he nodded thoughtfully. 'I understand now. He's very protective, isn't he? I asked him to introduce us once and he refused point-blank.'

Petra looked up in surprise. 'He did?'

'Yes, he did.' A smile lit his dark eyes. 'Mind you, I can't say I blame him. Are you two engaged, or anything?'

'No, certainly not. I told you, he's just a friend.' Petra found she was annoyed that Toby had taken it upon himself to manipulate her life like this. He was just like all the others who thought they knew what was best for her. 'Toby is just a friend, that's all. He had no right to...' She checked herself. 'I can make my own decisions.'

'Then prove it,' he challenged. 'Decide to have dinner with me – tomorrow?'

The direct challenge took her by surprise. His eyes held hers and she paused, her lips parted as she searched her mind for an answer. But before she could find the words he reached forward, cupped her chin and kissed her swiftly. Their lips brushed once, briefly, then with equal swiftness his arms went round her, drawing her close, and he was kissing her in earnest. When at last he released her she was breathless and trembling.

Holding her shoulders firmly, he looked into her eyes. 'I expect you're going to tell me I shouldn't have done that.' His eyes teased her gently.

'You think I'm naïve?'

He shook his head slowly. 'I think you're lovely, Miss Witching Hour. Well, are you going to have dinner with me tomorrow, or have I blown my chances?'

She smiled tremulously. 'I – think I might be going to have dinner with you tomorrow,' she told him gravely.

He raised an eyebrow. 'Only think?'

'All right – I'd like to. And thank you for asking me. But don't get any wrong ideas about me, James. I made up my mind a long time ago, even before...' her hand rose involuntarily to her face '...that men would play a very minor part in my life – if any at all.'

He pulled a wry face at her. 'Oh, dear, that sounds ominous! Any particular reason?'

'None that I particularly want to go into. I've seen other people make a mess of things through becoming too dependent on others. I had – I *have* my career. I intend to stand on my own feet. If there are any mistakes in my life, I'll make them by myself, then I'll have only myself to blame.'

James looked at her ruefully. 'Those sound like dangerously strict and simplistic parameters to set yourself. But, as you say, it's your life.' He opened the car door and got out. 'Thanks for the lift, Petra. I'll have my car back tomorrow, so I'll pick you up about seven. Right?'

'All right, fine.' She watched as he walked into the house. The encounter left her feeling strangely light, almost as though a weight had been lifted from her shoulders. For the first time for as long as she could remember she felt almost happy. Then suddenly she heard a bang – followed by a long wail. There was a staccato popping sound, like distant gunfire, and the sky above was scattered with the jewel-bright stars of a rocket. The spectacle reminded her sharply of another November night – of excruciating pain and terror. She shuddered and pulled up the collar of her coat, heading the car towards home. If she needed something to bring her down to earth, that was it.

The following day Petra spent most of the morning at the Bridgemount School, taking her dance team through its paces. She had decided that they should put on a Christmas show for the rest of the school; an impulsive decision she was having cause to regret as each successive rehearsal became more chaotic than the last. Petra had split them into three teams: one to do a Red Indian dance, complete with costumes which they were making themselves; a second to perform a simple mime and ballet from a story the group had devised between them. And the third, all boys, were rehearsing an energetic football routine. It was mainly this last that was causing Petra problems. The boys wanted it to be as realistic as possible,

which involved introducing some hooligan-
ism. Choreographing this for them in a way
that satisfied their need for realism took all
the creativity she could muster. After
supervising their enthusiastic rehearsal that
morning she felt exhausted and suggested
that they break for a rest.

It was while she was drinking a much-
needed cup of coffee that one boy sidled up
to her.

'The football dance is good, innit, miss?'

'Yes, Jason. It's coming along very well.'
She reflected wryly that at least the children
were enjoying it.

Jason eyed her speculatively. 'Miss, you
got a feller?'

She looked at him in surprise. 'Why do
you ask me that, Jason?'

''Cause if you ain't, c'n I be 'im?' As she
stared at him he added gravely, 'Oh, I know
you're quite old, miss, but I don't care about
that. I'm ten. How old're you?'

'Er – quite a lot older than ten,' she said,
trying not to smile. 'By the time you're
grown up I'll probably be a granny.'

He looked at her askance. 'Ger'on, you
ain't *that* old. I'll be seventeen in six n'arf
years. I'll be workin' by that time. Will you
go out with me then?'

'Well, you might have to remind me nearer the time, but I'd be honoured,' she told him solemnly. 'Thank you very much for asking me, Jason.'

'S'all right,' he said with a swagger. 'I like older women.'

The rest of the morning went with a swing. After the break Petra even managed to maintain reasonable discipline with the football routine. She congratulated herself that she was at last establishing a good rapport with the children. When she had first started to work with them they had been obstructive and aggressive, but now they were responding to her favourably – even seeing her as one of themselves, as Jason had just proved.

But as the day progressed there was one persistent doubt nagging at the back of her mind. Had she made the right decision in agreeing to have dinner with James? And as the evening drew closer she found herself becoming more and more nervous at the prospect. The last man she had allowed herself to trust had been Charles Bennett, and that decision could hardly have been more disastrous.

Before she went home that afternoon she looked in at the hospital with the tapes she had prepared for Jenny. For half an hour she sat at the little girl's bedside in the Intensive Care Unit, playing the tape of the children's voices over and over, holding Jenny's hand and talking to her, but there was no response. Sister had told her that Jenny's condition was stable. She had maintained the improvement made the previous day and was still breathing unaided, but apart from that there had been no further change. Finally, dropping a kiss on the little blonde head, Petra left. If only Jenny would regain consciousness! If only she could know that there was someone with her – someone who cared.

She was walking along the corridor, head down and deep in thought, when someone touched her arm.

'Petra.'

She looked up. 'Oh, Toby!'

'I tried to ring you last night,' he said. 'We really should record some more pro-grammes. I've got quite a lot of requests and other material for you.'

'Oh, fine. I was out last night, Anna and Ewan invited me to dinner.'

'I see. Look, Petra, there's something I wanted to ask you. Do you have time for a cup of coffee?'

'Well...' She looked at her watch. She didn't want to have to rush to be ready at seven. 'I can spare ten minutes, I suppose.'

His eyebrows rose. 'You can spare ten minutes, eh? Well, I'll try not to keep you,' he said with a hint of irony.

In the canteen he explained his plan. 'We're thinking of putting in a drama slot. I've found a couple of short plays with small casts – written by a friend of mine, actually, so no royalties to pay. And I thought we'd do a pilot – see how it goes, what kind of feedback we get.' He grinned. 'You know what our public is like! They'll soon let us know if they don't like it. The thing is – would you be willing to take part?'

Petra found her interest aroused. 'Yes, I'd love to, Toby.'

He grinned. 'Great! I thought you might. I'll pop round this evening with the scripts, shall I? I'd like your opinion on those too.'

'Oh – no, not this evening. I'll be out.' Why did she feel so guilty about it? she asked herself resentfully.

Toby looked puzzled. 'Out two nights on the trot? You *are* getting busy! I'll soon have to make an appointment to see you.'

'It was only the other day that you were complaining that I didn't mix enough!' retorted Petra.

He stared with dismay at her pink cheeks

and glittering eyes. 'I'm only joking, love. I'm glad you're going out and enjoying yourself, of course I am.' He waited. And she knew he expected her to tell him where she was going. When she didn't he said awkwardly, 'Right, I'll bring the scripts round tomorrow, shall I?'

'Yes, that would be fine, Toby.' She stood up, glancing once again at her watch. 'I'll have to go now. See you tomorrow. Bye.'

That evening, as she got ready for her date with James, Petra couldn't shake off the memory of Toby's wistful face as she left him in the hospital canteen that afternoon. It irritated her that she should feel so guilty. She and Toby were friends, nothing more. She owed him a lot, but she wasn't answerable to him for her every move. So why did she feel like this? And why did he have such a low opinion of James? The answers came swiftly: he did not approve of James because he was afraid that he might hurt her; his concern was only for her. Perhaps she would have been wiser to have listened to his warnings.

After making up her mind about what to wear, and changing it several times, she finally decided on a black velvet skirt and crisp white blouse with a high frilled collar, dressing her hair in the style that had become almost second nature to her, the right side sweeping forward across her cheek. When she was ready she sat down to wait. James was late. She sat on the edge of a chair for ten minutes – which stretched into fifteen, and then twenty. She got up and began to tidy the room, nervously plumping cushions and stacking magazines. Clearly Toby had been right: James was unreliable. She should never have agreed to have dinner with him. She must have been completely mad to believe that...

The loud knock on the door abruptly cut off her angry thoughts. She straightened her back and for a moment stood still, the book in her hand halfway to the bookshelf. The knock came again, and she thrust the book in among its fellows, smoothed her skirt and went to the door.

James stood outside, an apologetic half-smile on his face. 'I'm sorry, Petra. Just as I was going off duty an emergency came in – a ten-year-old child who'd broken his femur falling off a playground swing. The poor kid was in shock and his mother was in a state too. I had to stay and see it through.'

'Oh, I see. Of course. Come in.'

He watched her collect her coat, his eyes

on her face. 'You were angry,' he said. 'You thought I'd stood you up.'

She shook her head. 'No, of course not.'

He stepped forward to hold her coat for her. 'Doctors are always having to let someone down, I'm afraid. Usually the people who matter most to them. It's an occupational hazard. Am I forgiven?'

Petra shrugged, forcing a laugh. 'Naturally.' She made to turn towards the door, but he held her arm.

'Petra, has Toby been telling you things about me?' Telltale pink colour confirmed his suspicions. 'Ah, I see he has. No, don't say anything – I'll draw my own conclusions.' He looked into her eyes. 'I'll just say this: few of us are what we allow the world to think we are. But I'm sure you know all about that, don't you?'

'Yes, I suppose you're right.'

'I know I am.' He opened the door and held it for her. 'Shall we go?'

The restaurant James had chosen was out in the country, on the Saltmere road. A long drive led to Mallingford Hall, which had been a Tudor manor house. The food was excellent and there were enough other diners to give it atmosphere, without being crowded. After they had eaten they moved into the lounge for coffee. A huge log fire burned in the inglenook fireplace, and James led the way to a settee pulled up close to it. As a matter of habit, Petra made sure that she seated herself on his right-hand side. It was quiet, warm and relaxed in the lounge. A waiter brought coffee, poured it for them, then discreetly withdrew. For a moment they sipped it in silence, then James said, 'Tell me what made you give up your acting career.'

Petra turned to look at him. 'You're joking!'

He looked surprised. 'Why should I be joking? I know you said you found it superficial...'

'That's right, that's what I said. But now you know the *real* reason, so why ask?'

He frowned. 'You're wrong – I don't know the real reason. I'm asking because I'd like to.'

She sighed. 'Please, James, let's not play games. Let's not pretend that the scar on my face isn't blatantly obvious. I have learned to live with it, you know. I don't need empty flattery. I was obliged to give up acting because I couldn't think of a single director who'd give work to an actress with a badly scarred face.'

He shook his head. 'Petra, I'm beginning

to wonder just where this scar you speak of is.'

'Please don't.' She gave an impatient little sigh.

'I meant that it seems to be more in your mind than anywhere else.'

'In my *mind?*' She stared at him indignantly.

'Yes, in your mind. Don't you ever look at yourself in the mirror? Oh, I know you must comb your hair, put on make-up and so on. But do you really *look* at yourself as I'm looking at you now?'

She bit her lip, lowering her eyes. 'It's not exactly what I enjoy most.'

'I thought not.' He put his fingers under her chin, lifting her face until she was obliged to look at him again. 'Why do you always contrive to sit on my right side, Petra? Did you think I hadn't noticed you doing that? And why do you carry your head in that particular way, and wear your hair forward?' As his hand gently drew back the heavy curtain of hair it took every ounce of her control not to draw away from him. She flinched slightly as she felt him touch her skin, but the warmth of his fingertips had a soothing effect.

Feeling her tension, he paused. 'Petra, as a

doctor I find myself constantly asking questions. Why do some things have to happen? What's the meaning behind some of fate's cruel irony? I don't have all the answers by any means, but one thing I have learned: it isn't what life deals out to us that matters, it's how we cope with it. It's what we make of the changes of direction we're sometimes forced to take. Some wear their scars like banners, use them to get sympathy; some learn things about themselves that they never knew before. Then there are those who merely hide behind them.'

'And you think I'm one of the latter?' She felt her colour rise as she swallowed hard at the lump in her throat. 'Perhaps you don't realise how it feels to have your confidence shattered, to be made to feel like a freak. It would be bad for anyone, but for me, who had a promising career to look forward to – one that depended on my looks...'

'"My face is my fortune, sir, she said."'

She flushed hotly. 'You're mocking me.'

James shook his head at her. 'No. You said yourself that what you were doing before seemed superficial. And by the way you spoke about your new career last night you're getting a lot more satisfaction out of what you're doing now. Others are benefiting too.

I've heard on the grapevine that you're good. You're getting results. I'm right, aren't I?'

Petra nodded. 'Yes. I love my work.'

'But there's a little part of you left over from your old life.' A little part called – vanity?' He took both her shoulders and shook her gently. 'Petra, can't you see – you have something much more valuable to offer now. Your own suffering has given you the compassion to feel for others. That's worth far more than a flawless complexion.' He tucked her hair behind her right ear. 'There – wear it with pride. Show the world what you're worth; that you've won through. It's how we feel inside about ourselves that makes us who we are, not what others think.'

Tears stood in her eyes as she looked at him. 'How do you know all this?' she whispered.

He smiled. 'As a doctor I've seen plenty of suffering. I've had my share of problems too. And I've had obstacles of my own to overcome. Maybe one day I'll tell you about them, but right now, our coffee is getting cold.'

Outside, the air was sharp with frost and there was a full moon. James had to scrape the frost off the car windscreen, but once they were on the road the heater made it warm and cosy. The conversation turned to lighter things. They discovered a mutual love of the theatre and music, and a passion for Chinese food. By the time they arrived outside Petra's flat their mood had lightened. As he switched off the engine she fell silent, wondering whether to invite him in for coffee.

'I'm afraid my flat isn't very much,' she said. 'No more than a bedsit really. But if you'd like coffee...'

'I'm afraid I'll have to go, love,' he said, looking at his watch. 'I promised to look in on the kid who broke his leg, so I'd better not leave it too late.'

'Well, thank you for a lovely evening, James,' she said.

'No – thank *you.*' He reached across and pulled her towards him. 'I hope I didn't go over the top earlier?'

She shook her head. 'Of course not. It was all true.'

'And the thing is, Petra, you're still lovely. This...' He bent towards her and gently brushed her right temple with his lips. 'This makes absolutely no difference to the way you are. If it stopped mattering so much to you, no one would even notice it.' As she raised her head to reply he covered her mouth with his and kissed her long and searchingly. Raising his head, he looked down at her. 'That was nice,' he said softly, smiling into her eyes. 'Very nice. But given, the time and the opportunity, we'll do better.'

CHAPTER SIX

When Toby arrived at Petra's flat the following evening she had supper already prepared. He looked at the table in surprise.

'I wasn't expecting this.'

'You mean you've already eaten?'

He shook his head. 'No. You know me – business first, food later.'

'You don't take proper care of yourself,' she said, putting a dish of piping hot lasagne and a bowl of salad on the table.

Toby grinned appreciatively. 'Well, any time you're volunteering to take me over...'

'I'm not!' She passed him a spoon. 'Just tuck in, then we'll get down to these scripts. Who's the author, by the way?'

Toby helped himself to a hot roll and reached for the butter. 'A girl I know. She's a special needs teacher and she takes classes a couple of days a week at St Cath's.'

'Oh, dear!' Petra pulled a face. 'An amateur, you mean?'

He frowned. 'She's good – you know I wouldn't entertain anything that was bad. She's had some work published – magazine stories and so on.'

'Mmm.' Petra applied herself to her food. 'Well, we'll see, shall we?'

'Perhaps you've got a better idea.'

She looked up at his sudden sharpness and saw that he was annoyed. 'Sorry, Toby, I didn't mean to criticise. This girl – is she a friend of yours?'

'In a way.'

She smiled. 'In what way?'

'She's – someone I've met socially once or twice.'

'You mean you've taken her out.'

He coloured. 'Well – yes.'

'Toby, there's no need to look like that. I'm glad you've met a girl you like enough to ask out.'

'Yes, I rather thought you might be.' He pushed his food round his plate for a moment, then, 'You and I – our – relationship, for want of a better word. It's never been more than platonic, has it?'

'No, Toby, though I do value your friendship. You know that.'

'Not enough to tell me you went out with James Ewing, though.'

Petra laid down her fork. 'Oh, Toby! It was only once. I would have told you if it had been important – and if I hadn't anticipated your disapproval. Look, he's a friend of Ewan's. He was there when I went to dinner the other evening.'

Toby was shaking his head. 'Look, you don't have to explain. You're not answerable to me. I tried to warn you about him, but in the end, of course, it's up to you.'

'Yes, Toby, it is, isn't it?' She passed him the bowl of salad. 'So now that we've got that out of the way, can we talk about the plays?'

He grinned wryly at her. 'Sorry – of course we can. I didn't mean to come the heavy. It's just that I worry about you.'

Petra cleared the plates away and brought in cheese and fruit. 'As a matter of interest, how did you know I'd had dinner with James, anyway?'

'Someone from the hospital saw you at Mallingford Hall. It was sheer coincidence.'

She watched as he made a pretence of enjoying his food. He looked so uncomfortable that she couldn't help feeling sorry for him. 'Tell me why you worry about me, Toby. Why do you think I need pampering?' she asked.

'I know how vulnerable and sensitive you are. You told me yourself about what happened in the past. I *care* about you, Petra. I couldn't stand by and watch you run headlong into another disaster, could I?'

'People aren't always what they want you to think,' she said, paraphrasing James. 'Sometimes there's more to them than meets the eye. A lot more.'

'They can pull the wool over your eyes, you mean...' He saw her expression and held up his hands in mock surrender. 'Sorry – sorry! Look, I won't say another word. I'm sure you know what you're doing – and what you want.'

When they had finished eating Toby insisted on washing up while Petra read the scripts he'd brought. To her surprise she found them very good and more than adequately written. One was a drama, the other a comedy, and by the time Toby returned from doing the washing-up she had looked at them both.

'What's the verdict?' he asked as he settled himself in the chair opposite.

'I think they're very good. In fact, I'd like to meet this...' she looked at the script again, 'Valerie Manners.'

'She'd like to meet you too,' Toby told her. 'She's another fan of yours.'

'It occurs to me that she might be persuaded to write some material for me – for the children to perform, I mean. Maybe we could work something out together.' Suddenly she noticed that he was looking at her oddly and asked, 'What is it? Why are you looking at me like that?'

'It's nothing – just that this is the first time I've heard you actually *ask* to meet someone new. What's happened to bring about the change in you?'

Petra shrugged. 'Maybe all you've been telling me over the past months has filtered through at last.' But in her heart of hearts she knew that James had done for her confidence in one evening what Toby hadn't been able to achieve in a year.

He looked pleased. 'I'm delighted to hear it. But what do you think about the plays? Which one do you think we should try for the pilot?'

'The comedy,' Petra said without hesi-

115

tation. 'What people in hospital want is a good laugh. And this...' she tapped the script, 'is it.'

They read the script through together and discussed who they could ask to play the other two parts. Petra brewed coffee while Toby made a couple of phone calls, and by nine o'clock they had the play cast and the first rehearsal date fixed. They both agreed that Valerie Manners should be invited to the rehearsal, which was to take place the following Sunday afternoon at Toby's flat.

It was eleven o'clock by the time he left, and Petra was getting ready for bed when the telephone rang.

'Hello.'

'Petra, it's me – James.'

'Oh – how are you?'

'Tired,' he said. 'I've been on duty for the past fifteen hours.'

'You should be getting some sleep,' she told him.

'I know. I just thought it would be nice to talk to you first. I'd like to see you again, Petra.' There was a small silence, then he asked, 'Is that such a terrible prospect?'

'No, of course not.'

'How about next Sunday, then? It's my day off.'

'Oh, I can't on Sunday, James. We're doing a play for Radio Cathy and I'm rehearsing.'

'All day *and* all evening?'

'Well, no. But there's someone I want to visit in the IC Unit – a little girl from Queen Matilda's Children's Home.' Petra had promised herself that she would go along in the evening, secretly hoping to be the first person Jenny saw when she regained consciousness.

'That's no problem. I'll pick you up there at – what, half-seven?'

'Oh, all right.' His positive manner took her breath away. 'Well, all right, James. Thanks.'

'I'll look forward to it. Sleep well. Goodnight, Petra.'

He hung up quickly, before she had the chance to change her mind, and she was left looking rather dazedly at the silent receiver.

James replaced the receiver. Petra could hardly be described as eager. It was obviously going to be necessary to take a firm stance with her. Given half a chance, she would have made an excuse to cry off. True, she had warned him that she didn't intend to allow any man to become too close to her. And yet he had believed that their dinner together had been a success. So much for his ego! Perhaps he'd gone over the top a little with his reassurance – appeared patronising. The thing was, he really did care about her. He'd surprised himself thinking about her on more than one occasion over the past few days. The way she had retreated into a tight little shell was positively tragic for a girl with so much to offer. But what he felt was more than mere sympathy. The feeling that was beginning to tighten its grip on him was something he hadn't experienced for a long time. The last time he had felt like this, pain and heartache had followed. He wasn't going to let that happen again, was he – *was* he?

Friday began badly. Petra overslept and was late arriving at the day centre. It had been raining all night and the morning was grey and cheerless. Mrs Bains, the cheerful lady who managed the refreshment bar, looked up as she came in.

'Mornin', love. You look like I feel – *'arassed*. No need to look at the calendar to know it's Friday the bloomin' thirteenth, eh?' She shook her tightly permed head, sending her dangling diamanté earrings jiggling wildly.

Petra struggled out of her mac. 'My alarm

clock didn't go off,' she said. 'And it was such a dark morning that I didn't wake. Anyway, I'm here now. Maybe we won't get many this morning.'

Mrs Bains chuckled as she pulled on her nylon overall. 'Don't you believe it, love. Mornin's like this brings 'em out like cockroaches out of the woodwork. Can't stand the thought of their own company of a dark, wet mornin'. Can't blame 'em, can you?'

She was right. Soon after nine they began arriving, some by volunteer cars, some by the special ambulance and some on foot. The cloakroom was soon steaming with wet macs and at the refreshment bar Mrs Bains did a roaring trade in teas and coffees. After giving them time to settle down Petra joined them.

'Good morning, everyone. It's nice to see so many of you here this morning.'

'Nuthin' else to do on a day like this,' came the answering remark from somewhere at the back of the room.

One old lady sitting at the front peered closely at Petra and nudged her neighbour. 'Who's she?' she demanded, cupping her ear.

'It's Miss Marshall, the thingy – you know – *therapist* person,' said the elderly man

119

sitting next to her in a loud stage whisper.

Mrs Gregory frowned. 'What's *she* want? 'Ere, it's not a Tupperware party, is it, or one o' them scanty underwear "do"s? I come 'ere for company and a bit of a talk.'

'And that's just what we're going to have this morning, Mrs Gregory,' Petra said firmly, recognising one of the regular grumblers. 'I thought we'd have a discussion first about television; talk about what you like to watch and what you'd like to see more of.'

Mrs Gregory gave a derisive snort. 'I know what I'd like to see *less* of,' she said vehemently. 'All that kissin' an' rollin' about in bed. Disgustin', I call it!'

'Speak for yourself,' said a jolly little fat lady at the other end of the row of chairs. 'I may be old, but I haven't forgotten how it felt to be young.' She giggled. 'I *like* the love stories.'

Instantly an argument sprang up. Some said there was too much sex on TV, others thought there was more violence, which was worse. Petra let them warm up for a few minutes, then she threw in another thought.

'Right, so if you could plan your ideal evening's viewing, what would you choose?'

The lively discussion that followed estab-

120

lished that the one thing that was popular with everyone was the soap operas. But there was an area of disagreement about which one was best.

'I don't know why they think we want to know about folks on the other side of the world,' said a grumpy old man sitting in the corner. 'Half the time I can't tell what they're saying.'

'That's 'cause all these Aussies *mumble* so,' Mrs Gregory told him. 'They're always leavin', too. Just when you get used to them, off they go and turn into bawlin' pop stars or something.' She shook her head. 'No, give me a good old English tale – like *Dynasty*.'

Petra opened her mouth to correct Mrs Gregory's mistake, but before she could do so half a dozen others had done it for her, also pointing out that the programme she mentioned had its fair share of steamy love scenes. But Mrs Gregory would have none of it.

'Oh, I do the tricky bits of me knittin' when the love bits is on,' she said dismissively. 'An' if it's not English, then why is it full of English actors? Just you tell me that,' she challenged. 'Anyway, *I* like it.' Having pronounced her verdict, she sat back and folded her arms in a gesture that told them there was no more to be said on the subject.

'Right, then, if you could have a brand new soap opera, what would it be like?'

Petra's challenge silenced them for a moment, then a timid little old lady at the back said, 'I'd like one about the war – not the fighting but the way it was for us ordinary folk.'

This seemed a popular idea, and soon the room was buzzing with ideas. One old man announced that he had a scrapbook, and promised to bring it along; others had photographs, medals and newspaper cuttings. Petra suggested that they might create an exhibition. The suggestion was seized upon enthusiastically, and by lunchtime they had already made plans. Petra would borrow some screens and their souvenirs would go on show to the public in the foyer of the day centre. Some were even planning to get together in their own homes to choose the items that would go on show. What had started as a dreary wet morning finished with all the old people chatting animatedly as they went off to collect their coats and wait for their various forms of transport.

As Petra went to collect her coat Mrs Bains looked up from her washing up and winked at her. 'Got 'em goin' all right this mornin', love, didn't you? Talkin' about the war is the one thing they *all* like. I reckon you've hit on a winner there.'

Toby called for Petra early on Saturday and they spent the morning doing the rounds of the wards for the Christmas request show. The patients thoroughly enjoyed it. There was an air of light-hearted gaiety about St Catherine's this morning, especially in the children's wing where decorations were already going up and the Christmas spirit was getting off to an early start. In fact, Toby's jokes, antics and funny faces got the children so excited that Sister warned him that she would have to ask him to leave if he didn't curb his enthusiasm.

At lunchtime they went off to the canteen, where Toby had arranged for them to meet Valerie Manners. Petra liked the girl on sight. Blonde and pretty, she was effervescent with energy and enthusiasm, and full of ideas for the Christmas programme.

'I'm looking forward to sitting in on the play recording,' she told Petra. 'I've always wanted to hear one of my plays come to life, and I'm so glad you agreed to play the leading part. You have just the right kind of voice.'

After lunch Petra said goodbye to Toby and Val and went along to see Jenny. Intensive Care was quiet and still after the bustle of the canteen and the excitement of the morning on the other wards. The staff nurse shook her head when Petra asked if there was any change. Sitting beside the bed, she opened her bag and took out the cassette machine and began very quietly to play the tapes. Taking one of the small limp hands, she gently chafed it in her own, speaking softly to the unconscious child.

'Jenny, wake up for me, darling. Everyone's waiting for you, you know. It'll be Christmas soon. Down in the children's ward they're putting up the decorations. There's a tree too, with tinsel and coloured lights, and a fairy on the top with a real magic wand. I wish you could see it! Hurry up and get better so that they'll move you down there, then you will.' She stopped speaking to study the little face. Had she seen the eyelids flicker, or was it her imagination? 'Jenny, can you hear me, darling? Please wake up for me!'

There it was again. The eyelids half opened, closed again, then opened. Jenny's blue eyes gazed, unfocused, at Petra. A little frown wrinkled her brow for a second and her lips moved. Petra leaned forward to catch the word the child was trying to say.

'Yes, darling, what is it?'

The small hand that lay in hers curled tightly around her fingers and, in a small husky voice Jenny said one word.

'Mummy.'

Petra bit her lip. 'No, darling, it's...' But the eyes had closed again. With the familiar, heartrending little lopsided smile on her lips, Jenny had sunk back into oblivion.

Petra looked around for a nurse, but there didn't seem to be one in sight. In the corridor she was just in time to see James coming out of the lift. He smiled when he saw her, but the smile faded quickly as he caught sight of her anxious expression.

'Petra, what is it?'

'It's Jenny. I was playing tapes to her – and talking, when suddenly she opened her eyes. I think she may have recovered consciousness.'

He moved quickly towards the ward entrance. 'I'll have a look at her. You'd better get Sister.'

When Petra came back a few seconds later with Sister, James emerged smiling. 'It's all right, she's sleeping now,' he said softly, then to Sister, 'I only checked her as an emergency. You'd better get Mr Michaels to come

125

and take a look at her.' He took Petra's arm. 'We'd better go now and let them get on with it. I'm sure you can visit again tomorrow.'

In the lift Petra looked at him. 'There's something that worries me slightly,' she told him. 'When Jenny came round she called me Mummy.'

James smiled. 'I wouldn't worry about it. She's bound to be confused just at first. Next time you come she'll know who you are.'

But Petra was still worried. If Jenny was suffering from amnesia she would have to undergo the trauma of her parents' death all over again.

All the way down in the lift she worried. James didn't know the case as she did. She was so preoccupied that she failed to notice when they reached the ground floor, and James had to speak to her twice before she heard him.

'Petra, I said here we are. Aren't we speaking any more?'

She looked up with a start. 'Oh, sorry – I was miles away.'

He gave her a wry smile. 'So I noticed. How did your rehearsal go?'

She nodded. 'Oh, quite well, thank you. We've been recording on the wards for the

Christmas request programmes too.'

'And now?'

'Now?' She was still miles away.

'What are you going to do *now?*' he asked.

'Oh, I see. Nothing, apart from a call I have to make at Queen Matilda's Children's Home. I want to tell them that Jenny has recovered consciousness.'

'Of course. Your car is here?'

'Yes, in the... Oh, *no!*' She suddenly remembered that Toby had given her a lift that morning. 'I had a lift in this morning. But it doesn't matter – I'll get the bus.'

'Don't be silly. It's on my way, I can drop you off. Or better still, wait for you, and then we can have something to eat.' James looked at her enquiringly.

She hesitated for a moment. 'Well...'

He took her arm and marched her towards the car. 'I'm taking that as a yes. Your trouble is that you think too long about everything.'

In the car she was silent, and James looked at her. 'Something still bothering you?' he queried.

'It's Jenny mistaking me for her mother,' she told him. 'Her parents were killed, you see. She'd come to terms with that. If this accident has made her amnesic again...'

He smiled and reached across to pat her hand. 'Don't worry – I'm sure it's just confusion, as I said. When she comes round properly she'll probably remember everything perfectly.' He paused. 'How did she get those burns, by the way? Not in the accident?'

'No. In the fire in which she lost her parents.'

'Poor kid! I take it she was treated for them at another hospital.'

'That's right. Matty's was the nearest children's home that could take her,' Petra explained.

'She's still wearing pressure garments, I noticed,' said James.

'Yes.' She glanced at him. 'The burns are why I feel a special affinity with her. Perhaps you guessed that.'

He didn't reply, but after driving in silence for a moment he said, 'I'm sure Bates-Nicholson would be interested in her case. He's particularly interested in burns.'

Petra's head spun round to stare at him. 'Mr Bates-Nicholson? The consultant you're going to be working with? Is he a...?'

'Plastic surgeon? Yes.'

'But – but when I was treated here it was by a Mr...'

'Grimshaw,' he supplied. 'He retired last year.'

'Oh, I didn't know.' But there was no time to pursue this disclosure further, for James was turning into the gates of Matty's. Petra got out, slipping in to pass on the good news about Jenny. She kept her own small worry to herself, hoping that James was right and that Jenny would remember everything next time she wakened. Back in the car James looked at her.

'All right?' he queried.

'Fine, thanks.'

He switched on the ignition. 'Right, back to my place, then. I've got a very nice spaghetti bolognese in the freezer. A quick twirl in the microwave and we can eat.'

'I don't want to put you to any trouble,' she protested.

He laughed. 'Don't worry, I'll let you wash up if your conscience is bothering you.'

For the rest of the drive Petra was quiet, mulling over the discovery that James had ambitions in plastic surgery. Could his interest in her be purely clinical? Perhaps he didn't see her as a woman at all – just a test case.

The house James shared with two other doctors was a three-storey Edwardian villa, requisitioned by the hospital for its young resident doctors. What had been a large and beautiful garden had been mainly laid to lawn at the back and the forecourt concreted into a parking area. James unlocked the front door and led Petra up the stairs to the first floor flat. It was large and spacious, with two rooms, and a neat kitchen. Petra looked around with approval.

'This is nice. It makes my place look like a hovel.'

He was taking the bolognese sauce out of the freezer. 'It's not bad. At least we don't have to share a bathroom. They put showers in, it saves a lot of time.' He filled a saucepan at the sink and tipped spaghetti in.

'Can I do anything?' asked Petra.

'There's a bottle of wine opened in the fridge. You can pour us a couple of glasses. You'll find them in there.' He pointed to a cupboard.

They ate their supper sitting at the breakfast counter. Petra was surprised to find that the sauce was homemade and quite delicious. She said so, and James laughed.

'No place for the helpless male in today's society.'

'But there are plenty of convenience foods on the market,' she pointed out.

He pulled a face. 'Most of them take almost as much time as the real thing anyway. They're full of chemicals or "E" numbers too. Give me freshly cooked any time.'

'Some lucky lady is going to find a good husband some day,' she joked.

He shook his head. 'I think not. I've only been down that road once. Never again!'

She looked up at him, her fork halfway to her mouth. 'I see. Like me.'

He shrugged. 'Maybe. But we're not here to talk about that, are we? We have to let these things die a natural death.'

She paused. 'Is that how you come to earn the title of hospital Lothario?'

James laughed. 'Is that true?' He gave her a rueful smile. 'I suppose I do flirt,' he admitted. 'But only because it's a safe option. I prefer not to be taken seriously.' His hand reached out to cover hers. 'And I only tell that to exceptions to the rule.'

'How many of those are there?' she smiled, beginning to feel more relaxed with him. After a moment's thought she said, 'James, do you think Mr Bates-Nicholson would be interested in me?'

He laughed. 'Extremely so, I'd say. As long as his wife didn't catch him.'

'No, seriously. In my scar, I mean.'

He sighed and shook his head at her. 'Not in the *least*. He likes a challenge, and your scar wouldn't offer him that at all.' He plugged in the coffee machine. 'Shall we take our coffee into the other room? We could have some music and relax a little.'

'And what about you?' Petra stood behind him as he put cups and sugar on to a tray. 'Do *you* find me a challenge?'

He turned and looked at her. When she caught the look in his eyes she shook her head. 'Oh, no, I meant my burns – my scar…'

'Forget burns, Petra.' As she began to move away he caught her shoulders and drew her towards him. 'Do I find you a challenge? Yes, I do. Because I think that accident locked something away in you. My challenge is to release it.' He bent his head and kissed her, his strong arms drawing her close, his hand pressing the small of her back against him till they were as close as they could be. His lips were firm and insistent, and she felt her senses begin to sing as they hadn't done for a long time. Closing her eyes, she let herself relax in his arms, gave herself up to the headiness of his kiss, allowing her hands to find the nape of his neck and the strong hair that grew in surprisingly gentle curls there.

The tip of his tongue parted her lips experimentally, and she allowed this too, responding – feeling the room begin to spin. When he released her she was trembling, but she tried not to let him see.

Laughing shakily, she said, 'The coffee will be getting cold.'

He reached for her again. 'Damn the coffee! Come here.'

Petra took a step backwards. 'I – think we'd better drink the coffee, don't you?'

His eyes held hers. 'What are you afraid of, Petra?'

She shook her head. 'I'm not afraid.'

'No? Stay with me, then. Stay the night?'

Challenge. Now he was challenging her. Was it all a game to him? He'd said he didn't want to be taken seriously. Was he exploiting her insecurity – taking advantage? She took a deep breath and turned to pick up her coat. 'If you wouldn't mind, James, I'd like to go home now,' she said.

To her surprise he smiled. 'All right,' he said gently. 'All right, Petra, you win – *this time.*'

CHAPTER SEVEN

The run-up to Christmas was hectic for Petra. What with visiting Jenny, organising the exhibition at the day centre and rehearsals for the concert at Bridgemount School, she hardly had a minute to herself. She was grateful that she and Toby had recorded a batch of *Witching Hour* programmes as Valerie's play had taken priority over the past couple of weeks. It was now almost ready for recording.

Since the evening they had had supper together at his flat Petra hadn't heard from James. She had half expected a call from him, and when it hadn't come she had toyed with the idea of ringing him, but somehow she never quite summoned up the courage. The last thing she wanted was for him to feel she was chasing him. In spite of her hectic workload she found her thoughts returning to him again and again, so when the telephone rang one evening shortly before Christmas just as she was going out, she hurried back hopefully to answer it. She had been halfway down the stairs when she heard it begin to ring, and it had been a race to get back before the phone stopped ringing.

'Hello,' she said breathlessly. 'Petra Marshall speaking.'

'Hi, stranger. It's Anna.'

'Oh – Anna. Hello.'

There was a pause at the other end, then Anna said, 'Er – do I detect a certain little note of disappointment? Were you expecting a call from someone else?'

'No, of course not.' Petra forced a laugh, wishing not for the first time that Anna didn't have that uncanny sense of perception. 'I was just on my way out and I'm out of breath, that's all.'

'Mmm – well, I'll believe you. Look, I'm ringing because I wondered what you were doing for Christmas.'

'Well, nothing much...' Petra had refused an invitation from Anna and Ewan last year, feeling that they'd only asked her because they didn't want her to be alone. 'But you needn't worry about me,' she went on. 'To tell you the truth, I've been so busy I'll be quite glad of a chance to put my feet up.'

'I wasn't worrying about you,' Anna told her bluntly. 'Though now that you mention it, I can't think of anything more boring than spending Christmas with your feet up. Listen – Mary Fraser, Ewan and I are planning a reunion of Maltings patients. We've invited Megan Rees and her husband, Paul and Frank, George and Freda, and they've all accepted. Maude is full of ideas for the catering, and she and her husband are moving into my old flat over the holiday period to help. It's all going to be such fun!' Anna paused to let the plan sink in. 'You'd be the only person missing, so naturally we want you to be there too, Petra – to make the reunion complete.'

Petra chewed her lip, full of misgivings. She was torn between a genuine desire to see her friends again and hear their news and a reluctance to stir up old memories of a time in her life that she would prefer to forget.

Guessing at her thoughts, Anna said, 'It'll be marvellous to see how much they've all changed and improved, won't it? From what I hear, every one of you has made quite a significant success of your lives. I'm sure you'll all enjoy meeting again. Say you'll come, Petra!'

'Well, it sounds wonderful,' Petra said guardedly.

'Do you have another reason for not wanting to come?' Anna asked. 'Perhaps you're waiting for another invitation?'

'Oh no,' Petra said hurriedly. 'Look, obviously you'll be wanting to know as soon as possible, so...'

'You'll *come?* Great! Just wait till I tell Mary and Ewan. I told them you'd say yes. Can you be at Maltings in time for tea on Christmas Eve?'

'Well, I did promise to go into the hospital to see Jenny on Christmas Eve, but later in the evening...'

'That's fine,' said Anna. 'In that case, maybe you'd better come straight here to us. We'll have a late dinner together – say nine-ish. We'll be putting you up. Can you stay until the day after Boxing Day?'

'Yes, I suppose so...'

'Great! We're so looking forward to it all. So that's settled.' Anna sounded so excited that Petra abandoned up all hope of wriggling out of the arrangement. She'd been going to say that she'd think about it. But now it seemed she was committed.

At the beginning of Christmas week the cast of Valerie's radio play met at Toby's flat for the final recording. Listening to the tape as Toby played it back afterwards, they were all quite pleased with it, in spite of the inevitable post-mortems that ensued. As he packed away the tape, Toby told them that he had it scheduled for transmission in the first week of the New Year.

'So if you want to make any alterations, forget it. You're too late,' he added with a grin.

Later, as Petra helped him make coffee in the kitchen, he asked, 'What are you doing over the holiday, by the way?'

'Staying with Anna and Ewan,' she told him. 'There's a sort of reunion of former Maltings patients arranged, and Anna particularly wanted me to be there.' Looking up, she caught an odd expression on his face, just for a second she fancied it was relief. But she shrugged the thought aside.

'Have you heard from James Ewing lately?' he asked casually.

'No, not for weeks,' she told him. Suddenly she understood. He was relieved that she was going to Maltings for Christmas. That way she couldn't be spending any of it with James.

'What are you doing?' she asked. 'I dare say Anna would make you welcome too if you'd like to come.'

He shook his head, colouring. 'Oh, no, thanks. I'm planning to spend the entire holiday at Radio Cath's. Someone has to do it, and all the others have families.'

'Oh, Toby!' Petra felt a pang of guilt. 'I wish you'd told me – I'd have helped. Look, maybe even now I could...'

'No, don't be silly. Of course you mustn't cancel your plans. Anna would never forgive me.'

When it was time to leave Petra offered Valerie a lift. The other girl accepted and they left together. In the car Petra asked Valerie if she had any plans for Christmas. 'Will you be going away – visiting your family?'

'No. There's no one now,' Valerie said. 'There was just my father, but he died last year. And since my marriage broke up...'

Petra glanced at her. 'You don't see your ex-husband, then?'

Valerie gave a wry little laugh. 'Hardly – he's married again.'

'I see. So you'll be alone.'

'I would have been, but Toby has asked me to help him with the hospital radio shows over Christmas. I'm quite looking forward to it. It should be fun.'

The casually dropped piece of news pulled Petra up sharply. Why hadn't Toby mentioned it? Did he think she'd mind his spending time with Valerie? The irony of it struck her. When she'd told him she was going to Maltings she'd taken his odd expression for relief that she wouldn't be seeing James. I'm getting too self-centred, she told herself. People have their own lives to live. Why should anyone care what I do?

'Are you all right?' Valerie was peering at her.

Petra smiled. 'I'm fine. Just a bit tired – end-of-term blues. I'm sure you know all about that?'

'I certainly do,' Valerie nodded. 'I hear you're putting on a concert at Bridgemount School. That's quite an achievement. The children there are notoriously difficult to handle.'

Petra smiled. 'You're right there! More than once I've wondered if I'd bitten off more than I could chew. It's tomorrow night, actually. Come if you've nothing else planned.' She grinned. 'I can promise you that whatever else it is, it won't be boring!'

'Thanks, I'd love to.' Valerie was silent for a moment, then she said hesitantly, 'Petra – look, I know you and Toby are close friends. I hope I'm not – well, coming between you in any way.'

'Of course you're not,' Petra assured her.

'Toby has been a good friend to me, but there's nothing deeper between us.'

'You're sure?'

'Quite sure.'

Valerie sighed. 'Well, that's a relief. Since my divorce he's the first man I've found myself able to talk to. He's so sensitive and understanding, isn't he?'

'Very,' Petra agreed. 'After my accident I found it difficult to make friends. Even when I left the rehabilitation centre and began my drama therapy course I still felt that no one would really want to know me, with my disfigurement.'

Valerie turned to stare at her. 'Your *what?*'

Petra's hand went automatically to her face. 'This – my burn scar. I was badly burned in an accident at a fireworks party. When I was in hospital, just after it had happened, my hair had been burned too, and the way people turned away from me in embarrassment used to tear me up. I made up my mind then that I'd turn away first myself once I got out of hospital and spare myself the expression of pity on their faces.'

'It must have been awful for you,' Valerie said quietly.

'It was.'

'But now that you've had the plastic surgery you don't have that worry any more,' Valerie said brightly. 'It's wonderful what modern surgery can do, isn't it?'

Petra stopped the car outside the little house Valerie shared with a friend. She turned to look at the other girl. Was she going to be like all the others – playing the hateful charade of pretending the scar didn't exist?

'The scar is still there, and always will be,' Petra said crisply. 'It's all right, Val, you don't have to pretend. I've come to terms with it now – at least for now. I'm saving hard for some private treatment. That's why I'm still living in that poky little bedsit. But it's going to take a long time.'

Valerie shook her head. 'But surely there's no need, Petra? There's absolutely nothing to see. If I hadn't been told about your accident...'

'Been *told*?' Petra heard herself snap. 'Has Toby been discussing me?'

'*You* told me, Petra,' Valerie said patiently. 'Just a moment ago. Toby has only mentioned you in passing. He's certainly never said anything about an accident.'

Petra bit her lip. 'Oh God, I'm sorry, Val,' she said. 'Forgive me. I used to get uptight like that all the time. I thought I'd grown out of it.' She pushed a hand through her hair. 'I must be even more tired than I thought.'

'Forget it – I understand.' Valerie laid a hand on her arm. 'I was really touchy for ages after my divorce. I couldn't stop wondering if it was all my fault that Phil, my husband, had left me for someone else. I felt so unattractive, so inadequate and worthless. I can imagine what you must have gone through, even though it was a different set of circumstances.' She looked at Petra with sincere blue eyes. 'We are friends, aren't we?'

'Of course we are.'

Valerie looked thoughtful. 'Look, the girl who shares the house with me is getting married soon, and I won't be able to manage the rent alone. You wouldn't like to share with me, would you?'

Petra was tempted. To have a whole house – with a real kitchen and a bathroom she'd only have to share with one other person. It sounded like heaven. Then she thought of her slowly growing savings and shook her head. 'I'd love it, Val. But I really do need every penny I can save.'

Valerie looked disappointed. 'Pity, I don't know anyone else I can ask. But if you're really sure...'

'I am, but thanks for thinking of me. Look,

I'll pick you up tomorrow evening, shall I – about seven? I shall need all the moral support I can get, believe me?'

Valerie laughed. 'Right, I'm your man. See you then. Night!'

When Petra arrived backstage at Bridgemount School the following evening Mrs Crouch, the headmistress, met her. She looked harassed, her face flushed and her normally neat grey hair escaping wildly from its chignon.

'Oh, Miss Marshall, thank goodness you're here! I can't do anything with them,' she said despairingly. 'They're all so excited, they're like tightly corked bottles of pop. I'm afraid they'll explode in a minute.'

Valerie raised an eyebrow enquiringly. 'Want any help?'

Petra shook her head. 'No, I don't think they'll be in the mood for strangers. Both of you go and take your seats. I'll cope.' She gave them a wry smile. 'Or *not*, as the case may be! Just keep your fingers crossed for me.'

In the dressing-room the noise was deafening and chaos reigned. The cast of the football routine were fighting among themselves; the Red Indians were quarrelling over their

warpaint and the mime group had their costumes hopelessly mixed up. Petra clapped
her hands for silence.

'Quiet, everyone! Just calm down. There's
still plenty of time. Now what seems to be
the problem?' She held up her hands as the
children crowded vociferously round her.
'And don't all speak at once!'

Her presence seemed to have a calming
effect on them. The shouting and arguing
died down, and Petra set about sorting out
their respective problems.

The programme was to open quietly with
the mime, and when the time drew near
Petra ushered the little group into the
wings, making sure that all the others were
safely behind the closed door of the dressing-room, with strict instructions to stay
there until they were called. The teacher
who was acting as stage manager gave the
signal, the music began, the curtains parted.
The concert had begun.

The audience was spellbound, and the
children came off to encouraging applause.
Petra bundled them into the dressing-room
where the Red Indians, who were on next,
were waiting nervously for their turn. The
colourful routine was well received and, as
Petra had predicted, the football sketch was a

riot; though, to her relief, a controlled one. The boys remembered their moves perfectly and managed to refrain from putting too much enthusiastic realism into the 'violence'.

At the end of the concert the three teams of children took bow after bow, and finally Mrs Crouch led a reluctant Petra on to the stage and presented her to the audience. Later, when she rejoined Valerie, the other girl told her how impressed she was.

'I recognised one or two of those kids, having had them through my hands at an earlier stage,' she confided. 'And I can tell you that to get out of them what you did this evening you must have worked a minor miracle. Congratulations! What they've done tonight will have given them such a sense of achievement.'

Petra laughed. 'Not only *them*. I've even had one proposal of marriage,' she said. 'From Jason Smith, the thin, dark-haired boy who played the centre-forward in the football routine.'

'I'm impressed. You must have made a hit. I hope you didn't turn him down?'

Petra shook her head. 'Of course not. I've a feeling he'll change his mind by the time he's old enough, though!'

The evening ended with carols, followed

146

by coffee and mince pies, served by the 'actors', who had flatly refused to change out of their costumes and make-up.

Petra was tired by the time she got home, but just as she was letting herself in she heard a telephone ringing upstairs and realised it was coming from her own flat. Racing up the stairs, she rummaged frantically in her handbag for her key, flung the door open and almost fell into the room. But just as she reached out an eager hand for the receiver, the phone stopped ringing. Breathlessly she collapsed on to a chair. Damn! Now she would never know who was trying to ring her.

Christmas Eve on the children's ward was always fun, so Sister told Petra. At the far end stood a tall Christmas tree, shimmering with tinsel and glowing with coloured lights. Gaily coloured paper chains garlanded the walls and there was an atmosphere of suppressed excitement among the small patients. Before she went inside Petra had a word with Sister, asking about Jenny's progress. The little girl was out of danger and careful monitoring had shown that she had suffered no brain damage. But although she remembered Petra and all the staff and children from Tilly's, she still asked about her parents. It was as though the fire in which they had been killed and she herself injured had never happened.

'It often happens,' Sister said. 'Something as traumatic and unacceptable as that is often blocked out. Mr Michaels says the memory will come back in its own good time.'

'Has she asked about them?' asked Petra.

'She thinks they're abroad,' Sister said. 'Apparently they used to go away for quite long periods – something to do with her father's job. Jenny was looked after by an au pair.'

Petra shook her head. 'When she does remember, won't it be terrible for her?'

'Mr Michaels says that she'll remember when she's strong enough to accept it.'

'And when she is – and does?'

Sister shook her head. 'Who can say? Better to meet that when it happens.'

Jenny was in a bed at the far end, where she had been moved following her discharge from the Intensive Care Unit. As Petra walked down the ward towards the small solitary figure her throat constricted. All the other children had parents with them, in some cases brothers and sisters too. Only Jenny was alone, a small, pathetic figure, smiling bravely in an attempt to look happy.

'Hi there.' Petra dropped an armful of parcels on to the foot of the bed. 'And how's my favourite friend?'

Jenny's little face lit up, the wide blue eyes alight with the special smile that never failed to bring a lump to Petra's throat. 'Petra, hello. Happy Christmas.'

'Happy Christmas to you too.' Petra sat down on the bed and took Jenny's hand. 'The parcels are for you, but you must promise not to open them until tomorrow.'

'I promise,' Jenny said solemnly, her eyes straying curiously to the brightly wrapped presents at the foot of her bed. 'Will you be here?'

Petra shook her head. 'I'm afraid I'm going away tonight for a couple of days. But some of your friends from Tilly's are coming in to see you tomorrow, so you won't be alone.'

Jenny accepted this resignedly. 'Mr Michaels says I can go home soon after Christmas,' she told her. 'But that won't be till Mummy and Daddy get home, of course. He came to see me yesterday and brought another doctor with him.'

'Really? Who was that?'

'His name was Mr Bates-Nicholson, and he wanted to look at my burns. Mr Michaels

149

said he was the plas – plastic something.'

'Plastic surgery consultant? That's good, isn't it?'

Jenny frowned. 'I don't know. He won't hurt me, will he?'

'Good doctors never hurt you,' said Petra. 'Don't worry.'

'What will happen? Will I have to come back into hospital? What will they do to me?' asked Jenny anxiously.

Petra took both small hands in hers. 'They want to make sure that you grow up to be as pretty as you should be,' she said gently. 'I'll tell you a secret – I had it done.'

'*You* did?' Jenny's eyes were round.

Petra held back her hair. 'Yes. Just here, see? I was burned too, just like you.'

Jenny reached out to touch the scar tissue. 'Did Mr Bates-Nicholson do that?'

'No, it was another doctor,' said Petra.

'Will they make mine as good as that?' she whispered.

'Better,' Petra promised.

'And will I grow up to look like you?' Jenny settled back happily against her pillows. 'Wait till Mummy and Daddy come back and see how nice I look!' Before Petra could reply she went on excitedly, 'Did you know we're having some carols tonight? It's supposed to be a surprise, but Sister told me. Some of the doctors and nurses are going to come and sing for us.'

'That'll be nice.'

'Will you stay till they come?' The large blue eyes looked at her appealingly.

'Well, I will if it isn't too late.'

'It won't be too late. They'll be here soon. We've all got to be very quiet when they're singing,' Jenny added in a whisper.

Petra had saved up all her news to amuse Jenny, and she told her about the concert at Bridgemount School. She was just coming to the end when there was a sudden expectant hush in the ward. She saw all heads turn towards the ward entrance and followed their gaze to where the group of singers had just come in. They carried lighted candles and were dressed in long cloaks, the men in dark blue, the women in scarlet. The lights were lowered, then, singing 'Away in a Manger', they walked slowly down the ward in pairs to group themselves around the Christmas tree. As Petra watched she suddenly caught the eye of one of the male choristers, and her heart jumped. It was James – the last person she had expected to see.

Jenny tugged at her arm. 'Miss Marshall, look! That man there – the tall one. He came to see me with the other doctor I told you about yesterday.'

The group sang four carols, walking out of the ward as they had walked in, in pairs, this time singing 'Silent Night'. When they had gone, their voices dying away as they moved away down the corridor, Jenny looked tired and flushed. Afraid that she was getting over-excited, Petra tucked her up and kissed her.

'Off you go to sleep now,' she said gently, 'or you won't be bright and chirpy for Christmas Day. I'll come and see you again on Boxing Day. Be good and have a happy time, eh?'

Jenny nodded sleepily. 'Happy Christmas, Petra. And thank you for the presents.'

Out in the car park, a cold wind was blowing, carrying with it a few flakes of snow. Petra shivered as she stood beside her car, searching her handbag for her keys.

'Having trouble?' James appeared as if from nowhere, just as Petra had remembered that the keys were in her coat pocket and pulled them out. She promptly dropped them.

'Oh, *no!*' As she bent to look for them her head collided with James's. *'Ow!'*

He laughed as he put his hands under her

elbows and raised her up. Peering into her face, he said, 'Sorry. Did it hurt?'

'It's all right, I'm fine. It's just – my keys.'

'Here they are.' James dangled them on their ring in front of her nose, then took her hand and dropped them into the palm. 'How are you?' he asked.

'I'm fine, thanks. You?'

'Fine too. What do you think of Jenny? Doing well now, isn't she?'

'Yes, though she still hasn't remembered about her parents,' Petra told him.

'She knows who you are, though?'

'Oh, yes.'

He gave her arm a squeeze. 'Don't worry, it'll all come back in time. You're cold,' he said, feeling her shiver. 'Can we get into your car and talk?'

Inside the car Petra was acutely aware of his nearness, the familiar scent of his after-shave tantalising her nostrils as he leaned across her to switch on the courtesy light. He looked at her.

'That's better,' he said. 'I can see you now.'

Her eyes shifted from his intent gaze and she fiddled with the ignition key. 'Was there something you wanted to say?'

'Yes. I thought you might be interested to hear that Mr Bates-Nicholson is going to do

153

some further surgery on Jenny's face – try to release those muscles more.'

'Oh? That is good news.'

'I thought you'd be pleased. Petra, why haven't you been in touch?'

She looked up at him in surprise. '*Me?* I thought you...'

He shook his head at her. 'When you left the flat that night I got the impression that it was up to you whether we met again or not.'

'Well, yes, but...'

'We live in an age of equality, don't we? On that occasion you weren't ready to take our relationship further. I thought that perhaps when you were, you'd get in touch.'

She coloured. 'I'm sorry, I don't work like that.'

He smiled. 'Then how do you work?'

'I – don't know. I take things as they come.'

'I see. A step at a time?'

He was laughing at her and she resented it. 'I expect you're used to a more *liberal* kind of woman,' she sniped.

He winced. 'Ah, I suppose I asked for that.' Reaching out, he cupped her chin and turned her face towards his. His lips brushed hers once, then took them firmly. Petra submitted for a second, unable to resist, then she drew away.

'I – have to go,' she said shakily. 'I've got an appointment.'

'You're still afraid. Why? I told you, I'm not looking for a serious relationship – neither are you. What harm can it do to enjoy the attraction we feel for each other?'

She shook her head. 'I haven't thought about it. I don't even know that there is such an attraction.'

James regarded her, his dark eyes on her face until she could hardly bear it a moment longer.

'Oh, I think you do,' he said quietly. 'Suppose you think about it over Christmas and give me a ring afterwards, eh?'

'What? I'm not at all sure...' But he was already getting out of the car. He slammed the door shut and bent to look at her through the window. 'Merry Christmas, Petra,' he said. 'Take care. I'll be waiting to hear from you.'

CHAPTER EIGHT

Petra arrived at Hazelbridge with plenty of time to spare. Anna answered her ring at the doorbell with a smile.

'Ewan's still at the surgery,' she said. 'There's plenty of piping hot water, so why don't you take a lovely long bath to relax you?' she suggested, leading the way upstairs. 'I know you've had a hectic time, so you deserve a little pampering. Tell you what – I'll bring you up a nice long gin and tonic in about half an hour and we can have a lovely gossip while you dress.'

Petra enjoyed her bath. In the bathroom she found that her friend had laid out bath essence and a fluffy white towelling robe for her to use. Stretching out in the warm, perfumed water, she felt the strains and tensions of the day ease out of her, but as she lay there she couldn't shut out the memory of James's kiss or his casual words. 'What harm can it do to enjoy the attraction we feel for each other?' And really, why not? But she knew why not, even if she wasn't

156

admitting it to herself at the moment. Enjoying an attraction was playing with fire as far as she was concerned – at least, *this* attraction. Allowing James to amuse himself at her expense just wasn't on. There was no way she'd allow herself to be exploited again, however strongly she was tempted.

She had just returned to her room when Anna came in with two tall glasses on a tray.

'G and T for you, plain tonic for me,' she said, putting the tray down on the dressing-table. 'No more alcohol for me until after the baby.'

'You're looking marvellously well, and prettier than I've ever seen you,' Petra remarked. 'You're really happy, aren't you?'

Anna smiled. 'Happier than I deserve, I'm sure,' she said. 'Ewan and I just seem to fall more and more in love as time goes by. Sometimes I have to pinch myself to make sure I'm not dreaming. There was a time when I really thought I'd lost him for ever, you know.'

'When he was almost killed saving my life, you mean?' Petra said, wincing slightly at the memory.

But Anna shook her head. 'Long before that. It actually took that to bring us both to our senses, I think.' She smiled. 'We have a lot to be grateful to you for.'

Petra pulled a wry face. 'I only wish I could enjoy the credit. I must have been utterly impossible back in those days, and a terrible problem for you.' She picked up her hairbrush and began to brush her hair reflectively. 'And I'm not sure I've improved all that much.'

'How can you say that?' Anna asked in surprise. 'Look how well you've done. From what I hear you've made a fantastic success of your first term.'

'Oh, I'm satisfied with my professional progress,' Petra said with a shrug. 'It's personal relationships I still don't seem able to handle.'

'What about James Ewing?' asked Anna. 'I thought you and he were getting along rather well.'

Petra shrugged non-committally. 'We haven't seen each other for a while – at least, we hadn't until an hour ago.'

Anna looked at her curiously. 'You've seen him this evening?'

'Very briefly in the children's ward where he was singing with the carol singers, then later in the car park.'

'What did he say?'

'Just that Mr Bates-Nicholson is going to

operate on Jenny...' Petra broke off, glancing at her friend.

'Yes – *and*...' Anna prompted, sensing that there was more.

Petra sighed. 'I suppose you might as well know. James would like us to have a – well, a deeper relationship. And I'm not sure.'

'But you like him, don't you? Why aren't you sure?'

'Several reasons. I don't want to get too deeply involved, and I just might. I'm not the casual type.'

'Neither is James, I'm sure of that.'

'He says he doesn't want to be taken seriously,' said Petra.

Anna paused. 'I don't know, but I get the feeling that he's been badly hurt,' she said. 'He's probably afraid to commit himself again.'

'Well, that makes two of us, so why tempt fate?' Petra put down her brush and turned to look at Anna. 'I suppose if I'm honest I feel he might just think I'm a pushover because of my – my *affliction*.'

Anna stared at her for a moment, then shook her head. 'Oh, *really*, Petra, that takes the biscuit – even for you! *Affliction?* Petra, don't you know that when you love someone all their little – *imperfections* are part of

159

them? You love them too. No one can ever be perfect. How boring if they were!' She looked at her watch. 'Heavens! I'll have to go and see what's happening to the dinner.' At the door she paused. 'Look, it's only fair to tell you – I've invited James to dinner too. It was meant to be a surprise for you both, but I don't want it to be a shock.'

Petra spun round to protest, but already the door had closed. She turned back to stare at her reflection in the dressing-table mirror, taking a long hard look at her face with the bright hair drawn tightly back to reveal the pale creamy skin. If she were truly honest she had to admit that Anna was right. Although she could still see the hated scar perfectly plainly and knew that she always would, she had to admit that to the casual observer it must be barely noticeable now, even with her face devoid of make-up as it was now. She hadn't noticed its gradual fading in the passing weeks. The people she'd suspected of merely trying to make her feel better were telling the truth after all.

Suddenly she thought of the money carefully saved towards the private surgery she'd been planning. Her heart lifted. It wouldn't be needed now. She could look for a better place to live – she might even accept Valerie's offer to share the little house. She applied her make-up with extra care, then untied her hair and let it fall forward in its usual style. She paused to study her reflection, then suddenly she snatched up her comb and began to sweep the heavy chestnut mass up, away from her face, piling it on top of her head in the way she had often worn it in the days before her accident. Anna had said she was using her scar as an excuse for self-pity. Well, she'd show them all that she didn't pity herself any more.

When she was satisfied with her hair she stepped into the new dress and zipped it up. It was made of whisper-soft wool in a vibrant shade of aubergine that complemented her colouring dramatically. She paused to study the effect and decided that she had made a successful choice. She was just putting on the pair of creamy pearl earrings when Anna put her head round the door.

'James has arrived. He's downstairs,' she said briefly. 'Could you come down and entertain him for me? I'm still tied up in the kitchen.'

She withdrew immediately, and by the time Petra reached the landing Anna was already on her way downstairs. Leaning over the banisters, she hissed, 'Hey, Anna – does he know I'm here?'

Anna looked up with a smile. 'No. He has *that* pleasure to come.'

Outside the living-room door Petra stood for a moment, then she took a deep breath and walked in. James stood with his back towards the door, close to the fireplace in which a blazing log fire crackled. Petra's heart quickened as she watched him. It was obvious that he hadn't heard the door open. She cleared her throat.

He looked round, startled, surprise and pleasure showing clearly on his face. '*Petra!*'

'Hello, James. It seems that Anna invited us both independently – as a surprise. It was meant to be a pleasant one.'

'It certainly is, for me anyway. Can I get you a drink?'

The door opened and Anna came in, carrying a dish of cocktail snacks.

'Sorry about the delay, but dinner won't be long now,' she said. 'Ewan's just come in. He's gone up to change – ten minutes ought to do it.'

James smiled at her. 'Fine. Can I have some of those?' He took a handful of tiny biscuits from the dish she held. 'I hope you don't mind. I'm starving! Somehow I missed lunch today.'

Anna shook her head. 'Doctors! How you don't all have chronic ulcers, I don't know.' Swiftly she whisked the dish out of his reach. 'No more now. You'll spoil your appetite, and I've gone to a lot of trouble over dinner.' She looked speculatively from one to the other. 'Well, if you'll excuse me, I'll get back to the kitchen. Ewan should be down any minute now and, if I know anything, he'll be as hungry as you obviously are!'

All through dinner Petra feverishly searched her mind for amusing, light-hearted things to say, but she could think of nothing that didn't sound forced and stilted. All her amusing anecdotes seemed to come out sounding stupid and fatuous. It was as though her brain had turned into a solid mass of wet cotton wool.

They were halfway through their dessert when James's bleeper sounded and, with an apologetic shrug, he rose and went into the hall to use the phone. A moment later, when he came back into the room, he was already pulling on his coat.

'Got to go, I'm afraid. A bad RTA has tied the other duty doctors up and they need me.' He smiled resignedly at Anna. 'Thanks for a super dinner. At least I had time to eat it!'

'Never mind. I think I'm pretty used to this kind of thing by now.' Anna began to clear the plates. 'Petra, will you see James out for me while I see to the coffee?'

As they walked out on to the drive together, Petra said, 'I didn't know you were on call.'

'Yes. Haven't quite finished with A and E yet.'

'I – suppose you'll be on call all day tomorrow too.'

'I'm afraid I am.' James was unlocking the car, but he turned to look at her. 'I suppose it's too much to hope that you might miss me?'

She laughed. 'Why would I miss you? I haven't seen you for weeks until tonight.'

'And whose fault is that?'

When she didn't reply he reached out and pulled her to him. 'I might be selfish, but I'd rather like to think I'm missed tomorrow while I'm beavering away. Maybe this will help.' He took her head between his hands and kissed her slowly and searchingly, drawing from her an involuntary little murmur of satisfaction. 'Put your arms round me,' he whispered urgently. She slipped her arms around his waist and laid her burning face against his chest.

'You'll have make-up all over your jacket

now,' she told him, and heard his laugh vibrate against her cheek.

'Who the hell cares about that? I'll put my white coat on over it and enjoy remembering how it got there,' he told her. He pulled back his head to look down at her. 'Well, *now* will you miss me?'

She laughed. 'All right, you win. I'll miss you.'

'And will you ring me soon to say you're ready to see me again?'

'Perhaps. I – can't promise.'

'Well, I'll make *you* a promise,' he said, pulling her closer as he looked down into her eyes. 'If you don't ask, I won't. It has to come from *you*, Petra.' He kissed her swiftly, then put her firmly to one side as he climbed into the car. 'Goodnight, love. Have a happy Christmas.'

Petra sighed as she watched his car speed down the drive, breathing in the clear cold of the winter's night. In the distance she could hear a group of young carol singers, their voices raised joyfully in 'Hark, the Herald Angels'. The sound carried clear and pure on the frosty air, lifting her heart with it. She *would* miss James. Maybe being with him over Christmas would have helped her to make up her mind just how sincere he was.

She still couldn't quite forget all those stories she had heard about him. His kiss still warm and tingling on her lips, she walked slowly back to the house. And though she didn't know it, her eyes were shining as brightly as the stars.

As soon as Petra stepped in through the front door of Maltings next morning she felt as though she was coming home. The staff had been busy decorating and the hall was bright with gaily coloured garlands. In the corner near the foot of the stairs stood a Christmas tree sparkling with coloured lights and shimmering with tinsel. On the topmost branch was a large silver star.

As she, Anna and Ewan stepped in through the door, Mary Fraser came out to meet them. She held out her hands welcomingly to Petra.

'How lovely to see you,' she said with a smile. 'I've heard how well you've been doing from Anna, of course. And you look so well!' As she drew her close she searched Petra's face with perceptive eyes. 'It's quite amazing how your scar has faded,' she remarked quietly. 'I always knew it would, of course, but I'd no idea it would almost vanish. Congratulations!' She looked at the others. 'Now, I've invited one or two friends for drinks before lunch. There's Dr Phillips and Bill Hapgood – remember, our physio? Then there's Derek Graham and Leonie, his new wife.' She winked at Petra. 'I'm sure you remember Leonie.'

Petra did remember the young architect who had once dated Anna. And the lovely Leonie, who had been Ewan's fiercely protective receptionist when he'd been Dr Phillips' locum in the local practice.

'And – the others?' she asked.

Mary smiled. 'I thought you'd never ask! Yes, they're all here, in the lounge. I won't keep you from them any longer.'

Indeed, now that the moment had come Petra found herself becoming quite excited – almost shy at the prospect of seeing her former fellow-patients again.

In the large lounge, which was as gaily decorated as the hall, six people were waiting. George and Freda sat side by side on the window seat, looking for all the world as though they'd been married all their lives instead of just a couple of years; Megan Rees and her husband Jim were seated on the settee. Petra hardly recognised Megan. She had blossomed from the thin, haunted waif she had once shared a room with into a stunningly pretty girl, her shoulder-length dark hair shining and her eyes alight with happiness as she held her husband's hand. On the far side of the room Paul Blake sat puffing his pipe and beaming with pleasure. He too looked well, tanned from the open-air life he led at the successful garden centre and nursery he now ran. But the person Petra found she wanted most to see, the young paraplegic, Frank Harvey, Paul's partner, was missing. She greeted the others warmly and for a few minutes they exchanged news, but finally she could bear it no longer.

'Where's Frank?' she asked Paul. 'I hope he's all right.'

Paul grinned. 'You'll see in a minute.'

At that moment there was a loud pop and everyone cheered as Ewan poured champagne. Mary carried round the tray of glasses.

'Happy Christmas, everyone,' she said. 'It's a very special occasion for me, having my very first patients back again. And all looking so fit and very definitely rehabilitated.'

'A toast,' proclaimed Paul, raising his glass. 'To Sister Fraser. Without her none of us would be here today. And coupled with that – Mrs Anna Stuart, our hard-working occupational therapist who put us all on the right track.'

They all drank. Then suddenly the door burst open and the oddest Santa Claus anyone had ever seen trundled in. His 'sleigh' was a wheelchair and wisps of ginger hair poked out from under his white wig. On his lap was a bulging plastic sack which he was having difficulty controlling. When he spoke his voice was muffled by the copious false beard he wore.

'Ho, ho, ho! Happy Christmas, all,' he said. 'And for Gawd's sake will you all come and get your presents quick, before I drop this bloody bin bag?'

Laughing, they quickly relieved him of the sack. Petra bent to kiss his cheek.

'Frank, it's lovely to see you again. How are you?'

He blushed warmly, pulling off the cotton wool beard. 'I'm fine, thanks. How's yourself?' He shook his head. 'I don't need to ask, do I? You're looking great, gel.'

'So are you. In fact, everyone is. Wasn't this a lovely idea, having us all together again for Christmas?' She sat down beside him. 'Remember how we used to clash, Frank? I could have killed you at times, you were so damned rude.'

'You're a fine one to talk! What a pain in

169

the bum *you* were,' Frank said with characteristic bluntness. 'But I reckon you learned your lesson OK.'

Petra nudged him. 'It wasn't only me. You had a lot to learn too.'

'Yeah, I reckon you're right there,' Frank agreed. 'Remember when Anna let you take that drama therapy session? I made a right pig's ear out of that for you, didn't I? Poor old Anna! I don't know how she stood us sometimes.' He grinned at her. 'C'mon, then, tell us about your new job.'

She told him about the children at the Bridgemount Special School because she knew he would identify with them, and he laughed at her description of the concert she had produced.

'Tell you what,' he said. 'I'd love to meet these kids. Will you take me to see them over Christmas, Pet?'

'Oh, Frank, that would be marvellous! We could go tomorrow. You'd be a wonderful role model for the kids at Bridgemount. You've had so much to overcome, and you've done so well.'

'Ah, I've been lucky, though,' he said. 'I've had Paul and people like Anna and Sister Fraser to help me.' He gave her his cheeky grin. 'I reckon I must have done something good some time in my life to deserve the breaks I got.'

Petra felt suddenly ashamed. Compared to poor Frank, who would never walk again, she had so much; she was so lucky. And yet she still had a lot to learn. 'Frank,' she said thoughtfully, 'it's quite mild this morning. Shall we go out and have a look at your garden?'

He looked a little surprised. 'I've already had a look. Not much to see this time of...' He peered at her. 'What is it, gel – got something on your mind?'

'I just feel like a breath of fresh air – and your company,' said Petra.

The garden for the disabled that Frank had designed and built with the help of the other patients at Maltings had been the turning point in his recovery. It had led to his new career as Paul's partner in their garden centre project. As he sat with Petra, well wrapped up against the cold, he told her about his delight and fulfilment in seeing wasteland transformed into gardens on housing estates and – a recent triumph – the landscaping of a new pedestrianised shopping complex.

'I reckon I only got the contract because our tender was the cheapest,' he said modestly.

Petra shook her head at him. 'Rubbish! You got it because yours was the best and you know it. Congratulations.'

He grinned. 'Thanks. So you like your new job. Any fellers on the scene yet?' he asked after a pause.

'I do have a nice man friend,' she told him. 'Toby is his name. He's been very good to me – helped me a lot. You'd like him, Frank. He's a graphics designer and he works for the hospital radio in his spare time, like me.'

'Mmm...' He was watching her face. 'He's not the one who's bugging you at the moment, though, is he?' He touched her arm. 'Come on, gel. We didn't come out here to look at the scenery, did we? If you wanna talk, better get it off your chest before we both freeze to flippin' death!'

Petra sighed. 'You're right. He – James, that is – is a doctor, and we met because he used to listen to my hospital radio programme while he was on late duty. For a long time we just talked on the telephone. I wouldn't even let him see me because I thought I'd be a disappointment.'

Frank looked at her incredulously. '*You* – a disappointment? You're right, gel, you *are* an idiot!'

'We did meet eventually,' she went on. 'We

172

have a lot in common really. He changed direction – careers, just as I have. He's hoping to specialise in plastic surgery. At first I thought that must be why he was interested in me.' She smiled at him apologetically. 'I still don't have much confidence, Frank.'

'But now you know it's you he's interested in?'

Petra nodded. 'He doesn't want a serious relationship, but – and here's the problem – he does want more than...'

'He wants to sleep with you?'

'He's left the decision to me, that's the awful part.' She sighed. 'It's different for a man, Frank. I know we're supposed to be liberated and all that, but deep down I'm so afraid of being hurt again. I can't take these things lightly as some people can. I'm terrified of falling in love – that's the truth. And I don't know what to do about it.'

Turning, he looked into her eyes and saw the brightness there. Reaching out, he took her hand and squeezed it warmly. 'But it's too late, isn't it? You already do – love him, I mean?'

The question shocked her and she turned to look at him. 'I – don't know. I haven't let myself think about it.'

He gave her a wry grin. 'Oh, come *on*,

love, leave it out! You know it's true. It sticks out a mile.'

'Oh, dear! Does it? But we hardly know each other really.'

'What did that ever 'ave to do with it?' laughed Frank. 'Gawd knows I'm no expert, but I do keep the old mince pies open. From what I've seen, loving comes first and getting to know each other comes after. Sometimes it don't work out, but you gotta give it a go if you love someone, eh?'

'But supposing it's just – well, physical on his part?'

Frank shrugged. 'He sounds like a nice guy to me. He wouldn't make a fool of you. Anyway, he'd have to be a bit soft in the head not to fall for you. So it's up to you, gel. Is it a gamble worth takin', or isn't it?'

'Going to him – saying the words – goes against the grain, Frank. I'm not sure I can do it,' she said, with a hint of the old pride he remembered so well.

'Maybe he's just as scared as you are,' he said perceptively. 'I expect he just wants to be really sure before he makes a prat of 'imself.'

'Mmm...' With a sudden shiver, Petra stood up. 'Come on, I'm taking you in before you catch your death. I should never have brought you out here. It's colder than I thought.'

Frank reached out and very firmly removed her hand from his chair. 'Hey, watch it! I can manage, thanks. Don't start treatin' me like a kid or you'n me'll fall out again. An' just you think about what I've said. Don't just *talk* about it, *do* something about it. An' bloody quick, before he changes 'is mind.'

The rest of Christmas was spent eating and drinking the bounteous spread that Maude had put on and meeting old friends. After her talk to Frank, Petra felt much better and even managed to enjoy herself. On Boxing Day, after making a telephone call to Bridgemount School, she took Frank along to meet the children. He was an instant hit with them. They loved his bright and breezy manner and his pithy humour. He told them all about his own childhood in a children's home, about his accident and the way he had adjusted to disablement. Some of the questions they asked were so intimate and personal that they made Petra flinch, but Frank answered them all as honestly and good humouredly as he could, with a characteristic twinkle in his blue eyes.

On the way back to Maltings in the car he

said to her, 'You never told me you were engaged to one of the lads.'

She laughed. 'Jason, you mean? Oh yes. The moment he gets a job he's taking me out.'

He chuckled. 'So he told me. Proud as punch, he was. You've obviously done a great job with those kids. They never stopped talking about you and the concert you produced. It's given them a terrific sense of achievement as well as a lot of fun.' He glanced at her. 'I was watching you in there. You forget all about yourself when you're with them, don't you?'

She smiled. 'Yes. That's why I love working with them.'

'Then the answer's simple.'

She looked at him. 'How do you mean?'

For a moment he was silent, searching for a way to explain. 'One thing I've learned, Pet,' he said at last. 'Everyone has an insecure side. Everyone, no matter who, has something in their life that matters so much that they keep it locked up, safe inside. A scar, if you like. Only with most people the sort that can't be seen. The trick is to find it, and when you have, to respect it – try not to walk all over it.' He grinned at her. 'Remember when we were making the garden at

176

Maltings – trying to remember where we'd planted things – remembering not to disturb the tender little seedlings? Well, it's like that sometimes with relationships too. Planting the seedlings isn't enough. You have to care for them too.' He squeezed her arm. 'Doing that helped us all then, Pet, didn't it? It can help you again now if you let it.'

That evening Petra slipped away to visit Jenny as she had promised. Up in the children's ward at St Catherine's she found the little girl looking downcast.

'Hi, there,' she said brightly. 'Did you have a nice Christmas?'

Jenny made a brave attempt to smile. 'Yes, thank you. Thanks for the teddy,' she said.

'I'm glad you liked him.' Petra picked up the little bear and sat down on the edge of the bed with him, straightening the red bow around his neck. 'What have you called him?'

'Paddy,' Jenny told her. 'He's just like the one I had before I was burned in the fire. He was called Paddy too, but they never found him afterwards. I kept asking and asking for him, but no one ever brought him.' The big blue eyes looked up at Petra. 'Mummy and Daddy never came either.' There was a long pause and then she said in an almost inaudible whisper, 'They died, didn't they, Petra?'

Petra's heart gave a painful lurch and she drew the little girl into her arms, holding her close. She couldn't trust herself to speak for the tears that threatened, and her eyes were wet with tears. To think that it was her Christmas present that had triggered the memory! But the child in her arms wasn't crying. She just clung, the thin little arms tight and desperate around Petra's neck.

On the way out Petra passed through A and E, but she was too preoccupied to notice James, who was just coming out of a cubicle as she passed. Thoughtfully he watched as she made her way to the exit and disappeared through the doors. Had he overplayed his hand? he wondered. Would she ever come to him of her own accord?

Strangely enough, when he had accompanied Mr Bates-Nicholson on his ward rounds this morning, Petra's name had come up. They had been discussing Jenny Brown's case, and the consultant had remarked that facial burns were far more traumatic for a grown woman than for a child, who would have more time in which to heal and adjust.

'When I took over from George Grimshaw he told me of a case he'd had,' he told James.

'A particularly beautiful young actress called Petra Marshall – her whole life and a promising career in front of her. Burned in a fireworks party accident – bad second-degree burns down one side of her face. He did a marvellous job. I saw the photographs that were taken, both before and after – grafts and some later releasing. There was a good chance of further natural improvement too. But it's the psychological damage that we so often fail to see.' He'd looked at James. 'There's a lot more than surgical skill for a plastic surgery consultant to learn, you know. It's equally important to understand the mental anguish that this type of injury carries as it is to perform a successful operation. That poor girl had no family to help give her the love and understanding she'd have needed – possibly for years after.'

His words had haunted James all day. Petra must have been through hell, trying to pick up the pieces of her life and start again. And he'd thought he was being so clever, forcing her to make a commitment – to have enough confidence to take the initiative on her own. Why on earth *should* she come to him when he'd offered her so little of himself? How could he have been so brash?

CHAPTER NINE

The tiny flat seemed drab and claustrophobic after Anna and Ewan's spacious house, and as she unpacked Petra felt post-Christmas blues pressing in on her.

She and Anna had parted affectionately. 'I've had a lovely time,' Petra said. 'It was wonderful, seeing everyone again. Thanks so much for inviting me.'

Anna looked at her thoughtfully. 'I've caught you looking rather pensive once or twice over the holiday. You're not unhappy about anything, are you?'

'I am a little concerned about Jenny,' Petra confessed. 'I felt so guilty about the teddy-bear I bought her restoring her memory.'

'Don't blame yourself, love,' Anna said. 'It would have come back some time soon anyway. Anything could have done it. At least now no one will have the traumatic task of breaking it to her again.'

'She's being discharged tomorrow,' said Petra. 'Sister told me that Mr Bates-Nicholson won't start on her plastic surgery until she's completely over the trauma of the head injury. They're marvellous at Tilly's, I know, but it isn't like home, is it?'

'And there are no other relatives at all?' asked Anna.

'Not as far as I know. She'll be at Tilly's till she's in her teens – like Frank.' To her dismay, Petra's eyes filled with tears again and she turned away, busying herself with packing her luggage into the car boot. 'Well, I'd better go now. Thanks again.'

As Anna watched her drive away she shook her head. Either Petra was overworking or there was some deeper reason for her emotional state. She was very much afraid that she could guess what that reason was. Without betraying Petra's confidence she had spoken to Ewan about it only last night, but he had advised her firmly against interfering.

'You know what Petra's like, darling,' he said. 'She's always had to work things out for herself. Surely you realise that by now?'

Anna did realise it, but it still didn't stop her worrying.

The first week of the New Year was quiet. Many of the schools were still closed. Even the day centre hadn't opened up again yet.

After Petra had worked on preparation for the new term's work she spent the rest of her time going through a pile of poetry and requests that had been sent to her for future *Witching Hour* programmes. As Toby was busy with his own work, she helped him out at Radio Cathy too, standing in for him once or twice as disc jockey on his request programme.

It was later in the week that she rang Toby to ask if they could meet and go through the material she had received; the stock of programmes was rapidly running out and it would soon be necessary to record a new batch. Toby sounded pleased to hear from her and suggested she might call round for coffee the following morning. On arrival she was slightly surprised to find Valerie giving the place a thorough clean. She switched off the vacuum cleaner to let Petra in.

'Hi. Come in. Will you excuse me if I just finish dusting? I'm afraid we rather let things go over the holiday.' She laughed. 'Nutshells get everywhere, don't they? I've been fishing them out of the loose covers.' She stood looking around her. 'I've been saying to Toby, it's high time this room was decorated.'

Petra nodded. 'Toby never has time for things like that. My place could do with a lick of paint too, but I hardly think it's worth it. As a matter of fact Val, I've been wondering...'

But Valerie wasn't listening. 'I thought a nice Wedgwood blue would look good in here,' she said, 'picked out in white. And these loose covers will come up like new with a good wash. The material's good.'

'Valerie, about your offer to share the house when your friend gets married – I think I'd like to after all,' Petra told her.

Valerie's face dropped. 'Oh. Well, that would have been lovely, of course. The only thing is–'

'Coffee up, you two!' Toby shouldered the door open and came in carrying the tray of coffees. 'I hope you've remembered that the play goes out this afternoon. You will be at St Cath's to hear it, won't you? I'm hoping to go straight round the wards afterwards to get some instant feedback. Come with me if you like.'

Petra thought Toby was referring to her and she opened her mouth to reply, but before she could speak Valerie said, 'Sorry, love, I can't this afternoon. I have to go into school for a meeting – term begins again on Monday. But I'm sure Petra will want to be there.'

'Of course, I'd love to.' Petra looked at

Toby. 'I've brought along some of the material I told you about on the phone. Do you have time to look at it now?'

Valerie quickly finished her coffee and stood up. 'Well, I'll leave you to it. I'm just popping out to do some shopping, Toby. We've absolutely nothing left in the fridge. Even the turkey is finished! See you later.'

When she had gone there was an awkward silence. Toby reached for his briefcase and shuffled the papers inside it, his face pink with embarrassment.

'Toby,' Petra reached across to touch his arm, 'what's wrong? Is there something you want to talk about?'

He dropped the lid of the briefcase and met her eyes. 'You've probably guessed.'

'Val has moved in?' She raised an eyebrow at him and then laughed at his crestfallen expression. 'Surely it must be what you both want?'

'Oh, yes,' he said. 'It's just...'

'You're not worried about what *I* think? Toby, it's none of my business.'

'Val's friend is getting married, you see,' he explained, 'and she couldn't afford to keep on the house they were renting alone.'

'I know. As a matter of fact, she asked me if I'd like to share with her,' Petra said. 'I'd made up my mind to accept.'

'Oh.'

'But it doesn't matter. I'll find somewhere else.' She smiled. 'Toby, for heaven's sake don't look so guilty! You *are* happy, aren't you? Val certainly seems happy.'

'Yes – yes, of course.'

'Then that's all that matters.'

There was a small silence, then he said, 'How about you, Pet? Are *you* happy? Did you have a good time at Maltings over Christmas?'

'Lovely, thanks. It was wonderful seeing all my old fellow patients again.'

'And James – did you see him?' He looked searchingly at her.

'He was at Anna's for dinner on Christmas Eve,' she told him. 'But he was on call in A and E over the holiday, so I didn't see him again.'

'Well, maybe it's just as well. You know what I think of James Ewing.'

'Yes, I know.'

He looked at her. 'Are you – I mean, does it matter to you?'

'Not a bit. You know how I feel about heavy relationships.' Petra changed the subject by opening her own briefcase and drawing out a sheaf of letters. 'Look, here are the latest batch of requests. Someone has sent in a rather nice poem – I thought I might include it.'

When Petra left the flat that morning she couldn't shake off the feeling that she was closing the book on a chapter in her life. Toby had been a good and valued friend, but now that Val had moved in with him they would clearly see each other only as colleagues in future. She thought about the new relationship and wondered if Val and Toby were in love. If only she could take things as casually! She had thought a lot about James since the talk she'd had with Frank. And she had almost made up her mind to go to him – tell him she was ready for that next step. If she was hurt again, then so be it. Everything has its price, she told herself wryly.

That afternoon she and Toby sat in the studio on the top floor of St Catherine's, listening in to Valerie's play as it was being transmitted. When the half-hour was over Toby took off his headphones and looked at her enquiringly.

'Well? I think that went rather well, didn't you?'

'I always feel I could have done better,'

Petra said. 'But I suppose it wasn't too bad.'

He stood up. 'Right, I think we'll make a start on Women's Surgical. Shall we go?'

'You go on. I'll catch you up in a minute.' In the top floor bathroom she combed her hair and put on fresh lipstick, then picked up her bag and walked out into the corridor. She had to wait a few moments for the lift, and when it arrived the door opened to reveal one occupant.

'Petra!' James looked genuinely pleased to see her.

'Hello. How are you?'

'Great. Started my registrarship officially this morning.'

'Congratulations.'

'Petra – look, I'm glad I've seen you. There's something I wanted to say.'

'Oh? I can't stop now, Toby's waiting for me. We're doing some research into radio programmes. Ring me later.'

He caught her arm as she made to get into the lift. 'It won't take a minute. I just wanted to say I'm sorry.'

She frowned. 'For what?'

'For pushing you too hard. It was thoughtless. I should have known better.'

'Oh, but I was going to...'

'No,' he put a finger against her lips, 'you

187

don't have to say anything. I hereby release you from your promise. I forced you into it anyway. It wasn't fair.' The lift buzzer sounded furiously as an impatient passenger somewhere below held a finger on it. James pushed her inside. 'Better go now. I'll see you around. Bye, Petra, take care.'

Petra walked round the wards with Toby in a kind of daze. What could have happened to make James change his mind? Had he met someone else – someone who didn't take life so seriously, didn't keep him waiting around? She tried hard to force down the hurt that clutched at her heart. What a good thing she hadn't made a fool of herself! To think she'd almost revealed her feelings to him! She'd had a lucky escape, and she should at least be grateful for that.

As they were leaving Men's Surgical Petra noticed a distinguished-looking grey-haired man smiling at her rather wanly from his bed in the end bay. She went across to him.

'Good afternoon. How are you?'

'Pretty groggy, I'm afraid,' he said. 'Excuse me for not getting up, but they relieved me of my appendix in the small hours of this morning.'

'I'm sorry to hear that.'

He smiled ruefully. 'It took me by surprise. Terrible pain – sudden collapse, and the next thing I knew I was in here being carved up by some total stranger.'

'I hope you'll soon feel better.'

'Thank you. Are you a health worker of some sort?' he asked.

She laughed. 'Good heavens, no! I'm doing some research for the hospital radio. We like to know what patients think of the programmes we put out. Did you happen to listen to the play this afternoon?'

His eyes brightened with interest. 'Ah, I did indeed. And I thought it was very good.'

'I hope it didn't upset your stitches,' said Petra. 'We've had one or two complaints about that from patients who've had recent surgery.'

The man looked puzzled. 'Stitches? Oh, I see what you mean. No, I'm afraid I listened to it in rather a different way from most people.' He looked at her closely. 'If I'm not mistaken, you're the young woman who played the leading part – right?'

Petra smiled. 'Clever of you! Yes.'

'Not really – I have a trained ear, you see, and between you and me, you stood out like a rose among thorns. You have a very beautiful and memorable voice.'

Petra blushed. 'Thank you.'

'Not at all. You're trained, if I'm not mistaken.'

'Right again.'

'So you're a professional actress?'

'Well, no – a drama therapist. I began an acting career, but...' She paused, unsure of how to explain her change in career, but at that moment the ward sister appeared at the end of the bed.

'I'm sorry, Miss Marshall, but I shall have to ask you to leave now. Mr Gresham only had surgery yesterday, and he needs his rest.'

'I'm sorry.' Petra stood up. 'Goodbye, Mr Gresham. I hope you'll soon be feeling fit.'

He smiled. 'I'm sure I will, especially if you come and see me again!'

The week that followed was busy, and Petra was grateful for the fact. At Tilly's Jenny seemed to have settled down again. The other children were glad to have her back, and Matron had even arranged a little party for her, to which Petra was invited. Before she left Matron took her aside.

'Mr Bates-Nicholson wants to do more plastic surgery on Jenny's face in a couple of weeks' time,' she said. 'But I'm a little worried.'

'Why?' asked Petra. 'Do you have to give permission – in *loco parentis?*'

Matron shook her head. 'Not exactly. While the Browns' solicitor is still looking for possible relatives she's a ward of court. It's just that I can't help wondering if they're – well, I hesitate to say this, but *experimenting* on the child.'

'What makes you say that?' queried Petra.

Matron shook her head. 'Well, while she was in hospital they took a tiny piece of skin and they say they're growing it under special conditions to graft later.'

'I can assure you that's no experiment,' Petra told her. 'The reason they couldn't do skin grafts on Jenny's face sooner was that so much of her body was affected by burns. This is a new technique, but it certainly isn't experimental. She's very lucky. Mr Bates-Nicholson is interested in doing what he can for Jenny. I happen to know his registrar and he's an extremely eminent surgeon. You've no need to worry.'

Matron looked a little shamefaced. 'Oh, well, that's all right, then. I hope you can understand my anxiety. I don't mean to question their integrity, but the poor child has gone through so much, I couldn't bear to see her suffer any more.'

'You say the solicitor is making sure there are no other relatives,' Petra said. 'Is there still a likelihood of finding some, then?'

Matron nodded. 'They're still searching. It seems there may be some distant cousin in New Zealand. We're still waiting for news.'

Petra had just arrived home that evening when the telephone rang. It was Val.

'We're having a party here on Saturday evening,' she said. 'It's just an informal, come-as-you-are thing. You will come, won't you?'

'Well...' Petra searched her mind for an excuse and then realised that there was no longer any reason why she shouldn't go. Lately her evenings had been fraught with thoughts of James, her mind going round and round the question of why he had suddenly dropped her. It was beginning to feel like an obsession, and the four walls of her flat seemed to close in on her a little more each evening.

'Thanks, I'd love to come,' she said firmly. 'See you on Saturday.'

She was on her way down from the psychiatric wing on Friday afternoon and was passing Men's Surgical when she suddenly thought of Mr Gresham and her promise to visit him again. Just inside the ward entrance, at the nurses' station, she found the ward sister and asked if she might pop in for a few minutes. Sister smiled.

'Please do. He hasn't had any visitors, though he has spent a lot of time talking to people on the telephone.'

'How is he?' asked Petra.

'Doing very nicely. Did you know that he's a theatrical producer?'

Petra's eyes opened wide with interest. 'No, I didn't.'

'He was here to see a touring show at the Theatre Royal,' Sister told her, 'to watch an actress that someone had recommended. He was taken ill in the theatre and brought in as an emergency. My only problem with him now is to stop him working.'

Petra found Harry Gresham looking very different from the last time she had seen him. The colour had returned to his cheeks and he was sitting up in bed, horn-rimmed spectacles on his nose, working on a pile of papers. The telephone trolley was at the ready by his side. When he looked up and saw Petra approaching his face broke into a smile.

'Well, well, this *is* a lovely surprise! Pull up a chair.'

'You're looking very much better,' Petra

told him.

'Feeling it, too, though these people still insist that I'm not fit enough to go home.'

She eyed the papers strewn all over the bed. 'Maybe if you took things a little more easily?'

'No chance! Too much to do. Listen – Petra, isn't it? I've been thinking about you all week.'

She blushed. 'Really? I can't think why.'

'Oh, no? Look, I'm not making a pass at you,' he laughed. 'I've been listening to your late-night poetry programme – enjoying it very much. You told me that you began an acting career. Ever thought of going back into the theatre?'

'Not really. I put all that behind me some time ago.'

He opened a briefcase that lay on his locker and drew out a folder. 'I'd like you to read this script,' he said. 'No, don't say anything until you've read it a couple of times. Look specially at the part of Claire.'

'Mr Gresham...'

'Harry, please.' He smiled disarmingly.

'Harry – maybe I should tell you that I gave up my acting career when I suffered burns in an accident.' She turned the right side of her face towards him. 'You see the scar?'

He leaned forward and pushed his reading glasses on to the top of his head. 'Now that you mention it, I can *just* see something,' he said, narrowing his eyes. 'But surely you couldn't have let that put a stop to your career?'

'I was doing a lot of TV work,' she explained. 'The camera can be cruelly revealing.'

'But *this* would be a stage part. It's going into the West End. Look...' He counted on his fingers. '...We have a backer, a theatre, a first-class director and cast – everything except a leading lady. She has to be special, you see. I'm determined to get the right girl. It's crucial.'

Petra laughed. 'But how do you know I'd be any good? You don't know my work. For all you know I could be terrible.'

'I've heard you, remember,' he reminded her. 'I've got a gut feeling about you, Petra, and my guts never let me down.' He grinned. 'Well, they do, or I wouldn't be in here, would I? But seriously, don't you see – it's almost as though I was meant to come into this hospital to meet you. With the director we've got, your lovely face and dramatic colouring, that voice, like the singing of angels...' He kissed his fingertips in an extravagant gesture. 'It's Kismet. I ask you, how can we fail?'

Petra's head was reeling as she stood up. 'I'm going, Mr Gresham – Harry – *now*, before you completely turn my head! I'll read the script as you ask, but I make no promises. I'm a qualified drama therapist now, and I love my work. It's very rewarding.'

He spread his hands. 'So who's asking you to give it up? Just this one show, then you can come back to your therapy.'

She backed away, laughing. 'All right. As I said, I'll read it.'

'Come back on Monday? Promise?'

'Well, I'll return your script and tell you what I think. At least I'll promise you that.'

She sat up till two o'clock next morning reading the play Harry Gresham had given her, glad to have something absorbing with which to pass the long hours. When at last she laid it down her mind was buzzing. The play was good – *very* good. But the part of Claire was more than that; it was wonderful – the part of a lifetime. And he had offered it to her! It was beyond all the wildest dreams she had ever had in those far-off days when acting had been her only love. She drew the curtains and sat staring out into the darkness. Perhaps she should go back. She loved her work, but there were others who could do it just as well as she. She had allowed herself to fall in love again too, in spite of all her resolutions, and James had no use for her kind of love. There were others who could supply his superficial needs. But this – this was one thing that only she could do, something she had been chosen specially for. Apart from anything else it would be marvellous therapy.

That same evening, while Petra was at home reading the play, Toby and Val were having a drink in the Crown. A group of doctors from St Catherine's came in, and Val looked across to where they stood by the bar. Suddenly an expression of astonishment crossed her face.

'What is it?' asked Toby, following her gaze.

'That man over there – the tall, good-looking one with the group of doctors from St Cath's – I could swear he was...'

'Dr James Ewing,' Toby supplied. 'Don't tell me he's an old flame of yours?'

'Not of mine, of Sarah Thomas's, a teacher friend of mine. We were all teaching in the same comp at the time. They were engaged. Then James suddenly decided that he wanted to become a doctor. Sarah was furious – insisted it was just a fad, some kind of crazy obsession. You see, James and a friend had been involved in a bad accident. His friend was killed, and James couldn't get it out of his head that he might have saved him. Of course, it meant a lot of upheaval, and they were going to have to postpone the wedding for quite some time. Sarah didn't like that one little bit.'

'I see. What happened?' asked Toby.

'She tried everything she could think of to change his mind. When she saw that he was determined she dropped him like a hot brick – married the deputy head about six months later. A hard case, old Sarah.' Val continued to stare incredulously across the room at James. 'Well, well, so he made it after all, then. I must say he looks well on it.'

Toby frowned. 'Don't keep staring at him like that. He's conceited enough as it is!'

But he was too late. At that moment James turned and caught Val's eye. For a moment he looked puzzled, then recognition lit his face and he lifted a hand in acknowledgement. As he began to thread his way through the tables Toby groaned.

'Oh, no, he's coming over!'

James stood looking down at Val, his lips curved in a smile. 'Well, well! It's Valerie

Manners, isn't it?'

She laughed. 'It certainly is. What a surprise! I've been here almost a year and yet we've never bumped into each other before. I'd no idea you were here.'

'Did my training at St Cath's,' he told her. 'Qualified a little over a year ago – just started my registrarship.'

'Great. Where do you go from here?'

'I'm hoping to specialise in plastic surgery,' he told her. 'And I've been lucky enough to get on the firm of one of the best consultants in the country.'

'Good for you. Well done!'

'Your husband move here to work, did he?' asked James.

'No. I came to get away. My marriage is over, I'm afraid.'

'Oh, I'm sorry.'

Toby reached out to pull out the vacant chair. 'You'd better join us – I'll get another round of drinks.' He nodded towards the glass in James's hand. 'I take it you'll have the same again.' He moved off towards the bar, a resigned look on his face. By the time he returned James and Val were deep in light-hearted reminiscence about their teaching days. Val looked up.

'I've invited James to our little bash

tomorrow evening and he says he'd love to come,' she said. 'Isn't that great?'

'Yes – great.' Toby's resigned expression deepened.

'Bring a girlfriend too, of course,' Val added. 'If you have one.'

'Oh, he will have.' Toby cast a rueful look at James, who tossed back his drink and rose.

'Well, you'll have to excuse me,' he said. 'John Bates-Nicholson is giving a lecture in the med students' common-room this evening and I promised to be there.'

When he had gone Toby shook his head at Val. 'I wish you'd asked me first before inviting him.'

Valerie looked surprised. 'Why? He's a nice guy.'

'He might have been when you knew him, but he's gained the reputation of hospital Casanova since he's been at St Cath's.'

Valerie looked at him reproachfully. 'His break-up with Sarah hit him very hard. I dare say he prefers to keep his relationships light these days, especially with all the studying he's had to do.'

Toby looked at her. 'Sometimes keeping things *light*, as you put it, can be pretty hard on the other person. He and Petra had a bit of a thing going before Christmas, but I get the feeling that all isn't well, so having them at the same party is hardly going to make the evening go with a swing, is it?'

CHAPTER TEN

Petra arrived early at Toby's flat the following evening. When Valerie opened the door she handed her a bottle of wine and a tinful of savouries she had made for the party.

'My contribution,' she said as she took off her coat. 'How many are you expecting?'

'Oh, about twenty,' said Valerie. 'Any more would be a bit of a squash in here.'

Petra looked approvingly round the newly decorated room. 'You've obviously been working hard. It looks very nice. You've made a big improvement...' She smiled. 'To Toby's life too, I imagine. Where is he, by the way?'

'Couldn't find a corkscrew,' Valerie laughed. 'He's still hopelessly disorganised. He's just slipped downstairs to borrow one.' She looked enquiringly at Petra. 'Did you want to speak to him?'

'I came early to see if I could help. But I

would like a word with Toby,' Petra confessed. 'Something has happened. I'd appreciate his advice.'

Both girls were in the tiny kitchen, arranging the food on plates, when the door's slam and cheerful whistling heralded Toby's return.

'Petra would like a word, Toby,' said Valerie, looking up. 'Why don't you go into the studio before the others arrive?'

As he closed the kitchen door Toby looked mystified. 'What's up? I was hoping we could have a recording session tomorrow morning, but if you...'

'Tomorrow morning will be fine, Toby,' Petra assured him. 'No, it's nothing to do with that.'

'What, then – something wrong?'

'Not exactly wrong.' She sighed. 'I'm in a bit of a dilemma. A patient on Men's Surgical has offered me a part in a play.'

Toby grinned. 'Well, that's an original line, I must say! So what's the problem? You act for Radio Cath's, so why not some amateur dramatics too?'

'No, you don't understand. This is a part in a new play that's being put on in the West End. Harry Gresham is a producer.'

Toby looked doubtful. 'You're sure he's

202

not putting you on?'

'I'm positive. Sister had already told me. He's turning the ward into an office and disrupting her routine.'

'Well...' Toby sat down. 'What do *you* want to do, Pet?'

She sighed. 'I wish I knew. It's a marvellous part, the chance of a lifetime. Any actress would give her eye-teeth to play it.'

'So...?'

'Yes, but I'm not an actress any more, am I?'

Toby shook his head. 'I think in your heart of hearts you'll always be an actress, Pet,' he said. 'But you're doing a valuable job and you do have responsibilities now.' He peered at her. 'Are you sure you're thinking straight?'

'What do you mean – thinking straight?' she asked indignantly.

'I don't know – just a feeling,' Toby said evasively. 'It was just that I thought you and James Ewing were...' He shrugged. 'Oh, nothing. Take no notice of me. It's just that I wonder if you're thinking of doing this for the wrong reasons.'

'Like what?'

'Like using it as an escape route. Running away from things isn't the answer, is it?'

Petra smiled wryly. Toby was so perceptive. He knew her so well. There had been a
time when she'd bitterly resented the fact
that he seemed to be trying to manipulate
her life. But now that she was free to make
her own decisions, she longed to be told
what to do.

Toby was looking at her. 'I haven't
offended you?' he asked.

She smiled. 'No, of course you haven't.
Thanks, Toby, I'll give it some more thought
before I make a final decision. After all, I've
got all weekend.'

An hour later the party was in full swing.
Petra had been into the kitchen to refill the
diminishing trays of snacks. She was coming
back when she saw James on the far side of
the room. She stopped in her tracks as their
eyes met briefly. Then a blonde girl whose
face was vaguely familiar to her took his arm
and began talking to him. So she'd been
right: James had found someone else. That
was why he had 'released her from her
promise'. She found that she was trembling
and was annoyed with herself; even more
annoyed with Toby for not mentioning that
he'd invited James. But she was determined
not to let anyone see her embarrassment.
She carefully avoided the corner of the room

where James and his companion stood. Valerie was circulating at that end anyway. Putting the tray down on a table, she began to make her way back to the kitchen, but just as she reached the door a hand reached across her shoulder to open it for her. She knew instinctively without looking that the hand belonged to James, and to her discomfort he followed her into the kitchen and closed the door.

'I didn't know you'd be here.'

She felt his eyes on her but avoided looking at him. 'Why shouldn't I be here? You knew I was a friend of Toby's.'

'Yes, but I thought parties weren't your scene.'

'You're right, they're not. I just felt like a change, but I don't want to be an embarrassment.' She reached for her coat, which she'd hung behind the door, but James took a step forward and took it from her.

'What are you talking about?' he demanded.

'I understand everything perfectly now.'

He frowned. 'Understand? What?'

'Why you're so generously letting me off my promise.' She took her coat from behind the door and began to put it on.

'I don't know what this is about, Petra, but

205

if you're leaving because I'm here, please don't. I only looked in on my way to somewhere else anyway. I'll be gone in a minute.'

'I'm not leaving because of you. I only really came to help.' The fact that he was with another girl hurt intolerably, but she was determined not to let him see. She could feel the hot colour creeping into her face as she tried to snatch her coat out of his hand. He held it just out of her reach, and she found herself biting back tears of frustration at what she saw as his wanton cruelty. Desperately searching for something with which to divert his attention, she blurted impulsively, 'Perhaps you've heard that I'll be leaving here for good soon.'

It was his turn to look stunned. 'No, I hadn't heard. Have you been offered another drama therapy appointment?'

'No. I've been offered the chance of a lifetime – a part in a West End play. I'm accepting, of course. I'd be mad not to. It's very exciting!'

Visibly stunned, James let her take the coat from him, dropping his hands to his sides. 'I see. Well, congratulations.'

'Thank you.'

For a long moment he stood looking at her, almost as though he was seeing her for the first time. Petra did her best to meet his gaze without flinching. She'd expected to feel triumphant, but she felt only a dull pain in her heart. His gaze held hers and the ache grew and grew until she felt she could bear it no longer. She was just about to give in and look away when he said:

'So – when do you expect to start rehearsals?'

She shrugged in an attempt at nonchalance. 'I'm not sure – soon. Well, I mustn't keep you from your – friend. She must be feeling neglected. If I – don't see you again, I suppose this is as good a time as any to say – goodbye.'

'I suppose it is.' After a pause he held out his hand. 'Well, good luck, Petra. I'm really glad you've found what you wanted, though I must say I'm surprised.' As he looked at her she could feel tears thickening her throat. 'Jenny's to have the first of her ops next week,' he went on. 'It'll be a fairly long haul – painful and uncomfortable at times. She's going to need someone around to give her some love and encouragement. I had hoped that you might...' He broke off, shaking his head. 'I'm sorry, I shouldn't be saying this to you. You have your own life to lead – exciting new horizons opening up for you.' He reached for the door. 'Goodbye, then, Petra. Maybe when you're rich and famous you'll come back and sign autographs for us all.'

Her heart was thumping fast. It took every ounce of control to keep her features under control until his back was turned. As the door closed behind him she turned and gripped the edge of the worktop till her knuckles showed white, squeezing her eyelids tightly in a vain attempt to stop the tears from falling.

James made his way across the room to where Valerie was chatting to one of the cast from her soap opera.

'Sandra and I will have to be going now, Val,' he said. 'We're picking up Gerald, her fiancé, and going on to a concert. As he was working a late shift I asked him if I could borrow her as I had no one else to bring.' He smiled and held out his hand. 'Thanks for inviting me.'

Val looked at the tense lines around his mouth. She'd seen him look like that before. 'James...' She held on to his hand and leaned forward. 'Did I see you go into the kitchen after Petra?'

'Yes.'

'I hope everything's all right?'

'Oh, yes. She's just been telling me about the marvellous offer she's had. It seems she'll be leaving soon.'

Valerie looked shocked. *'Leaving?* Toby said she'd been offered – but I didn't know she'd actually made up her mind. Are you *sure?'*

'It's what she said. And she seems to be over the moon about it.' On the other side of the room Staff Nurse Sandra Hilton was trying to attract his attention by holding her arm above her head and pointing to her watch. 'Sorry, Val, I'll have to go. Say goodbye and thanks to Toby for me.'

Valerie found Petra in the kitchen, washing up used glasses. She looked pale and strained, as though she was having trouble hiding her feelings – even trying hard to keep tears at bay.

'What are you doing in here, Petra?' she asked. 'Come and join the party.'

Petra began to untie Toby's striped butcher's apron. 'I think I'd better be off now, Val. I'm not very good company this evening – I've got a lot on my mind.'

'Yes, and I think I know what. I've just seen James. He's left. I don't know if that makes any difference.' Valerie laid a hand on Petra's arm. 'Look, it so happens that James and I know each other from the old days when we both taught at the same school. We ran into each other a few days ago, quite by chance.'

Petra nodded. 'That explains it. I knew Toby wouldn't have invited him. There's never been any love lost between those two.'

Valerie perched on a kitchen stool. 'Maybe because he doesn't really know him as I do. Look, tell me to mind my own business if you like, but just how much do *you* know about James's background?'

'He told me he used to teach – and that when a friend was killed in an accident he started to think seriously about becoming a doctor.'

'Did he mention the sacrifice he made to attain that ambition?'

'No.'

'He was engaged to a friend of mine,' Valerie said. 'When Sarah knew she'd have to postpone her wedding plans, perhaps for a couple of years, she ditched James without a qualm and quickly married someone else. I happen to know it hit him very hard at the time, though if you ask me, he had a lucky escape. If she couldn't stand up to waiting for him she wouldn't have made a very good doctor's wife anyway. She should have been proud of what he was doing, but all she could think of was herself.' She shrugged. 'But then James didn't see it like that at the time. We never do, do we?'

Petra was reminded sharply of her own shattering disillusionment with Charles. Clearly she and James had even more in common than she'd thought. But she refused to show how shaken she was. Picking up a teacloth, she began to dry glasses. 'It was all a long time ago. It's obviously changed – hardened him.'

'Oh, no, not James,' Valerie said quietly. 'Life changes us all, but deep inside we're the same people, with the same vulnerabilities and half-healed wounds. *I* know that, and perhaps you should know it even better, Petra.' She stood up. 'I'd better get back to the party now.' At the door she paused. 'Sorry if I seemed to lecture you, Petra, but I just wanted you to know that there's more to James than he allows people to see. I know him and I can tell that you're important to him. He deserves some happiness.'

'Perhaps his new girlfriend will bring him that.'

Valerie shook her head. 'Sandra's his

friend's fiancée. Didn't you know that?'

Petra stared in dismay at the door as it closed behind Valerie. Why hadn't he told her? She'd seen the blonde girl before – with James and his friend in the Crown. She'd have remembered who she was if she hadn't been so upset. Now it was too late.

When Petra arrived for her recording session with Toby on Sunday morning he was concerned at her appearance. Her face was pale and there were dark circles under her eyes.

'Are you feeling all right, Pet?' he asked. 'Not sickening for flu, are you?'

'No – just sickening.' She tried to smile. 'I slept rather badly, that's all.'

'Any particular reason?'

'Oh, you know – decisions.'

Sensing her evasiveness, Toby busied himself with checking the studio console, and began flicking through a box of tapes to find clear ones.

'By the way, about the play?' he asked. 'Val told me you'd already decided.'

'I wish you'd told me you'd invited James to the party,' she said suddenly.

He looked up at her sharply in the act of adjusting his headphones. So that was it! 'I didn't – it was Val. Sorry if it was awkward. They're old chums, apparently.'

'Yes, she told me,' said Petra.

'Was it seeing him that made your mind up for you?'

'Good heavens, no!' She opened her briefcase and drew out the programme of poems she'd selected. 'Let's get on with it, shall we? I'm better working.'

The recording went well. Toby thought he had never heard Petra deliver poetry with such feeling. Her low, musical voice seemed capable of expressing every emotion from laughter to sadness, and she had chosen her material well. In a very short time four programmes were in the can. They broke briefly for coffee, chatting about everyday things; both of them aware all the time that they were carefully skirting round the problem that was heavy on Petra's mind.

Back at the microphone, Petra took out one of the poems she'd received in the post. Glancing up for Toby's signal, she began to read. The poem was called 'Summer's Gift' and was all about lost love. Her voice was filled with emotion as she read the beautiful lines.

In the control-room, behind his glass panel, Toby looked up. Petra's voice had trembled

213

effectively on the last line, but he knew instinctively that she wasn't acting. One look told him that he was right. She met his gaze with one of mute appeal, her green eyes made huge by the tears glistening in them. Switching off the recording machine, he came through into the studio.

'Shall we call it a day?' he asked gently. 'You're tired. We've got four programmes in the can.' He sat down opposite, waiting for her to regain control. 'Anyway, love, if you're leaving, these *Witching Hour* programmes will have to end anyway.' He began aimlessly to shuffle papers in a token attempt at tidying the studio. 'Isn't it odd how everything can suddenly change?' he said. 'One day everything's normal, then all at once – bingo! – nothing's the same any more.'

For Petra his words were the final straw. She buried her face in her hands and gave way to the terrible aching force of her tears. Toby watched, helpless and uncomfortable. When women wept he never knew whether to try and stop them or to let them cry it out. Both seemed futile and ineffectual. Reaching out a tentative hand, he touched her shoulder.

'Pet – Pet love, don't! Would it help to talk?'

She opened her bag and fumbled in it for a handkerchief. 'There's nothing you, or anyone else, can do,' she said, swallowing hard. 'You were right, I'm just tired.'

'Look, I know – come back to the flat. Val's doing a Sunday roast. There's bound to be enough for three.'

She took a deep breath and stuffed the sodden handkerchief back into her bag. 'No, thanks, Toby. I'll be fine.'

'I don't think you should be alone,' he said worriedly.

'I won't be. I'm going to see little Jenny at Tilly's – she's going into hospital next week for her op.'

'Will you be here to see her through that?' asked Toby.

Petra began to gather up her things. 'I don't know yet. I do have a life of my own, you know, Toby. I can't let my emotions rule my life. That's why...' She broke off, seeing his surprised expression. 'Oh, come on, let's get out of here.'

She was glad to get into her own car and escape. Kind as Toby was, she couldn't confide to him the turmoil that was in her mind. She was having enough trouble understanding it herself. Suddenly she felt as she had felt when she first went to Maltings –

cast adrift, rootless; a terrible feeling of not belonging.

When she arrived at Tilly's Matron drew her to one side.

'There's been a development,' she said in a hushed tone. 'The solicitor who's dealing with Jenny's parents' estate has had some news from the agency he'd engaged to look for the cousin in New Zealand that Jenny kept talking about. They've found her. It seems she's on her way over from New Zealand to see the child.'

'Does Jenny know?' asked Petra.

Matron shook her head. 'I thought it best to say nothing to her just yet. She'll have enough to cope with, what with her operation and everything.'

'Do you have any information about this person?' Petra asked.

'Yes. She's married, but has no children of her own. She's Jenny's mother's first cousin and it seems the girls were once very close. But their parents quarrelled and they hadn't set eyes on each other since the cousin and her family emigrated. Mrs Anderson – that's her name – is very keen to see Jenny, apparently. She should arrive some time next week.'

'Well, keep your fingers crossed for Jenny,' said Petra.

She found the children playing quietly in the playroom and took Jenny for a walk, well wrapped up against the cold.

'I'm going to have my operation next week,' Jenny told her, looking up.

'I know.' Petra felt a pang of pity as she looked down at the little girl's cruelly scarred face.

'I'm glad you'll be there – and Dr Ewing,' said Jenny, slipping a trusting hand into Petra's. 'He's nice, isn't he?'

'Yes, he's nice,' Petra agreed.

'I asked him to make me look like you,' Jenny told her. 'And he promised to try.'

Petra hardly heard the child's chatter about what she had been doing at school. How could she leave and let her down? Suppose this cousin of her mother's raised the child's hopes, then went home and left her behind? She had yet to see how badly scarred Jenny was. Would she let the child's appearance put her off? Matron had said that the woman had no children of her own. Why was that? Perhaps she had never wanted or understood them. Who would be there to pick up the pieces for Jenny if she were to be upset yet again? Finally she was jerked out of her reverie by a sharp pull on her hand.

'*Petra!* I'm talking to you!'

'I'm sorry, darling. What did you say?'

'Are you staying for tea? We have cakes on Sunday – sometimes ice-cream too. Please stay!'

Monday was a very busy day, and it was quite late in the afternoon before Petra found time to visit Men's Surgical and Harry Gresham. She found him looking well, but impatient.

'I thought you'd never come,' he told her. 'They're letting me out tomorrow.'

'Oh, congratulations,' she smiled.

'Well?' He looked at her expectantly. 'What's the verdict?'

Petra took the script out of her shoulder-bag and laid it carefully on the locker. 'I love the play, Mr Gresham – and the part,' she said.

'What's with the *Mr Gresham?*' He narrowed his eyes. 'Does this mean you're about to turn it down?'

'Not exactly. What I'd like is a little more time. I'd have to give at least a month's notice, but there's another reason too.' She began to tell him about Jenny and her operation – the cousin who was arriving from

New Zealand and the doubts that she herself had about the situation.

'Are you always so concerned for others?' he asked when she had finished.

The question made Petra stop and think. She acknowledged that not so long ago her thoughts had all been for herself; she had been so full of self-pity. When she was at Maltings Anna had needed all her persuasion to get her to share her room with Megan – terrified out of her wits when a prowler had broken into her room.

'I used not to be,' she said at length. 'But it's part of my job now.'

His eyes softened and he reached out to grasp her hand warmly. 'Compassion is a rare quality in the theatre,' he said. 'It's such a competitive profession, as you know, and it's not always the nicest and the best who get the breaks.' He smiled. 'Have you lost your claws, little tiger?'

'I think I may have,' Petra confessed. 'Does it matter?'

'It might to you.' He regarded her for a long moment. 'Maybe there's another reason why you need more time,' he said, 'a deeper one. Look, I'll be gone tomorrow, but I'll give you my number.' He reached into his briefcase and produced a card. 'Ring me this time next week and let me know your final answer. It's pushing it, but I'll take the risk.'

'I'd hate to let you down, Harry,' she told him. 'Especially when you've offered me such a chance.'

'Don't worry about it,' he said, patting her arm. 'Just do what's right for you, then you'll be right for all of us.'

When Petra discovered the day scheduled for Jenny's operation she arranged her work so that she could take the day off. She arrived at the hospital at eight o'clock, just in time to hold Jenny's hand while she had her pre-med injection. Soon afterwards she looked up to find James coming into the ward. He wore outdoor clothes, and she guessed that he had just come on duty. It was raining outside and there were still raindrops glistening on his dark hair. The way her heart began to race when she looked up and saw him standing at the foot of the bed alarmed and dismayed her. When would he stop having this effect on her?

He seemed surprised to see her. 'Hello. I didn't expect to find you here.' He looked at Jenny. 'And how are you, young lady?'

Jenny gave him her lopsided little smile, but the medication was beginning to take effect and although she tried hard she found speaking too much of an effort. He turned to Petra.

'We're about to scrub up for the morning list, but I thought I'd just check on her first. It's good of you to come. How long can you stay?'

'As long as it takes. I've arranged to take the day off,' she told him. 'How long will the operation take?'

He shook his head. 'Quite some time. Immediately afterwards she'll spend quite a while in Recovery, then she'll have to spend a couple of days in the IC Unit. I'm afraid you're in for a long day. Why not go home and wait for a call?'

Petra shook her head. 'I promised to be here.' She glanced at Jenny, who was now sleeping peacefully. 'What are the chances she'll be as she was before?' she asked.

'If anyone can do a perfect job John Bates-Nicholson will,' he told her with confidence. 'Would you like to watch the op on TV from the observation-room? I think I can wangle you in with the students.'

Petra's heart gave a sickening lurch. 'I wish I could trust myself to,' she said. 'But with Jenny...'

He nodded. 'I know. It's different when it's

someone you know. I passed out cold at my first op!' he grinned. 'That took some living down, I can tell you, especially as I was years older than the other students. Look, how about meeting me for something to eat in the canteen at lunchtime? By then I'll be able to give you some first-hand information.'

'Thank you, I'd like that.' She watched him stride out of the ward, pausing at the nurses' station to speak briefly with Sister. He looked so assured and positive – a man who had given up so much to follow his chosen path. Suddenly she felt very small and inadequate.

Holding the small soft hand, she watched Jenny sleep, grateful that the child was at peace and beyond pain or anxiety. A lump came to her throat as she remembered the trust the little girl had in her and in James; the need she had for love and someone who truly cared.

When the porter came with the trolley and Jenny was gently lifted on to it she opened her eyes briefly and smiled at Petra.

'Are you coming with me?'

Petra glanced at the porter, who nodded assent. 'Yes, darling, I'm coming too.'

'And will you be there when I wake up?'

'I'll be there,' promised Petra.

As they walked along the corridor the porter said, 'You can come as far as the sterile area.'

'Thank you. And afterwards?'

'She'll come round in the recovery-room, but she won't know much about that,' he told her. 'She'll be going straight into the IC Unit after that. That's where you can see her.'

The hours seemed interminable to Petra as she sat waiting, a magazine lying unread on her lap. Finally the hands of the clock reached one, and a few minutes later the door opened and James appeared.

'Ready for some lunch?' he asked.

Petra rose to her feet and realised for the first time how stiff and tense she was. All morning she had scarcely moved. She searched his face.

'How is she?' she wanted to know.

'She came through the operation wonderfully well,' he told her. 'Bates-Nicholson did a fantastic job – released those taut muscles and grafted the skin we took when she was in earlier. I'm sure you'll see a huge improvement when the healing has taken place.'

Petra was almost overwhelmed with relief. 'How soon can I see her?'

'They'll be moving her to the IC Unit later this afternoon. You'll find her on a ventilator at first, because she's had facial surgery. She'll be sedated too, of course, so she may not know you're there. But in a couple of days she should start to make quite a rapid recovery.'

They found a table in the canteen and James collected their lunch from the counter. As he returned Petra said, 'Did you know that they've found a relative? A cousin in New Zealand. She's due to arrive any day now.'

'That's good.' He looked at her. 'It must be a relief to you. You must have been worried about leaving her.'

'Yes.' She pushed her food around her plate. 'I exaggerated a little at the party the other night. I still have to give Harry Gresham my final decision. I'd made up my mind to ring him this evening – after Jenny's operation.'

He looked at her. 'I see.'

There was an awkward silence as she looked out of the window. 'The rain has stopped,' she observed, acutely aware of his eyes on her.

'Petra...' his fingers touched hers across the table '...have you *really* thought this through? Are you sure you're doing the right thing? I know it's a chance in a million, but somehow I had the impression that you'd found your true vocation at last – and settled happily into it.'

She would have given anything to escape the dark, probing gaze of his eyes. 'So did I. But we can be wrong sometimes, can't we?'

He looked at her for a long moment, then: 'Look, Petra, maybe I'm out of order, but I've nothing to lose, so I may as well say what I think. I'm terribly afraid you're accepting this offer for all the wrong reasons. You're taking a step backwards, trying to fit yourself back into a broken mould, and I just wish I knew what prompted it. It's like me going back to teaching because I'm offered a headship when I know damned well that I can be a much better surgeon.'

'But I'm not like you,' she said, putting down her knife and fork. 'And anyway, what makes you think you know me? Maybe I *want* to be rich and famous after all. Maybe I need to prove my own worth – to *myself*. Maybe I'm sick of other people letting me down.' Even as she was saying it, it sounded pathetically inadequate. 'I'm not the dedicated type, like you, James,' she went on. 'And I can't make casual relationships.'

There was a silence that crackled the air between them like electricity, and suddenly Petra's meagre appetite evaporated. The sight of the food on her plate filled her with an almost overwhelming nausea.

'I wish I understood that last remark, Petra.' James shook his head. 'I thought we had more than a casual relationship. And just for the record, I don't go in for them either, whatever rumours you might have heard.' He reached for her hand and held it firmly. 'I happen to think you *are* like me, Petra. In the past I was afraid to be hurt too, but I took a chance. I hoped you might do the same.'

Something in his tone, some urgency, made her look up at him and his dark eyes held hers almost hypnotically. Then suddenly he glanced at his watch and shook his head with frustration. *'Damn!* I've got to go. Look, can I see you later? There's so much more I want to say, and this is neither the time nor the place.' He screwed his paper napkin angrily into a ball. 'I'm not telling you to come, I can't make you do anything. It's up to you.'

'All right,' she said softly. 'I'll be with Jenny in the IC Unit. I'll wait for you there.'

He rose from the table and stood looking

down at her. 'I'll pick you up when we've finished the afternoon list. You'll wait?'

Petra nodded. 'I'll wait.'

CHAPTER ELEVEN

When Petra first saw Jenny lying in her bed in the Intensive Care Unit she was reminded of when the child was in hospital following her accident. It seemed so soon for her to be back here. James had been right; she was heavily sedated, yet it was as though something told her that Petra was there. As she stood looking down, the child opened her eyes, smiled, then settled back into sleep.

It was lonely, sitting in the warm, heavy atmosphere of Intensive Care, and Petra's mind was in turmoil. Why hadn't she told James that she had still to make the final decision about Harry Gresham's offer? Somehow lately she didn't even understand her own motives any more. As she sat there, her thoughts tangled and confused, her eyelids became heavy. She must have fallen asleep for a moment and was startled when she felt a touch on her arm. It was

227

the staff nurse.

'Miss Marshall, I'm sorry to disturb you, but there's a lady here who says she's Jenny's aunt.'

'Of course.' Petra got to her feet and followed the nurse out of the ward. A woman stood in the corridor. Petra guessed her to be in her mid-thirties, tall and slender, fair-haired, like Jenny.

'This is Miss Marshall,' the staff nurse said.

The woman smiled, holding out her hand. 'Hello. I'm Fiona Anderson.'

Petra took the hand. 'I'm so glad you're here.'

'The Matron at Queen Matilda's has told me so much about you,' Fiona Anderson said. 'I'm so grateful for all you've done.'

'I haven't done much. Jenny is a very easy little girl to love,' said Petra. 'I'm afraid she's still barely conscious, but I'm sure you'll want to see her.' She glanced at the staff nurse. 'You're aware of what she's had done?'

'Yes.' The woman looked hesitantly at her. 'Before I go in could we talk for a moment?'

Petra was surprised. 'Of course.'

In the waiting-room Mrs Anderson sat down next to Petra. 'When we heard about the tragedy – my cousin and her husband's

228

terrible death – we were shattered. We weren't even aware that Margaret was married or that she had a child. Right away we decided, my husband and I, that we'd like to adopt little Jenny. I can't have any of my own, you see. Jenny would at least be close to me.'

'That's wonderful,' Petra said. 'But how can I help?'

'You know the child. From what I hear you've formed a close relationship with her. Do you think we'd be right to take her away from the country where she was born – away from all her friends? We're family, of course, but we're also total strangers to Jenny. Would it be fair, or even wise? We only want what's best for the child, you see.'

Petra had taken to the woman almost on sight and, seeing her concern and sensitivity, she had no doubt that Jenny would take to her too.

'I believe that what Jenny needs more than anything is love and a secure home, Mrs Anderson.' Petra went on to tell Fiona Anderson about Jenny's accident and the temporary amnesia that had forced her to come to terms with the loss of her parents for a second time. 'She's a wonderful little girl, Mrs Anderson,' she said. 'She has such patience and courage. Any family would be proud to call her their own. If you can spare the time, why don't you stay on until she's out of hospital – take her away for a holiday and get to know her?'

'That's a wonderful idea!' Fiona Anderson beamed. 'I could get Larry, my husband, to come over and join us. We could have such fun, the three of us.' She stood up. 'I'd like to go and see her now.' She hesitated. 'Will you come with me – just so that she knows I'm not really a stranger?'

Jenny was awake when they returned to the ward. Petra bent down.

'Jenny, this is your Auntie Fiona – your mummy's cousin. She's come all the way from New Zealand to see you.'

She moved aside so that Jenny could see her visitor. The child's eyes lit up and she held out her arms, and Petra saw that there were tears in Fiona Anderson's eyes as she bent to the child.

Quietly walking out into the corridor, Petra drew out the card that Harry Gresham had given her. She'd go and ring him now. What she had just witnessed had confirmed her decision.

In the surgeons' changing-room James

stripped off his gloves and greens and dropped them into the bin. The hot shower revived him, loosening his stiffened muscles. As usual he ached from the long hours of concentration. He was assured that he'd grow used to it, but the blissful relief after a long day in the theatre was, to him, only part of the satisfaction he achieved from working with a brilliant surgeon. As he watched, he promised himself that if one day he could be even half as good as John Bates-Nicholson, he would consider all the hard work and the sacrifices well worthwhile.

As he dressed in his outdoor clothes he thought of Petra. The thought of seeing her and saying what was in his mind made him hurry, buttoning his shirt and tying his tie as quickly as he could. The afternoon list had been a long one. Looking at his watch, he saw that it was already a quarter past five.

'Coffee and sandwiches are waiting in the surgeons' room, Doctor,' Theatre Sister told him as she bustled past him in the corridor. But he shook his head, hurrying towards the lift.

'Thanks, Sister, but I have an appointment.'

When she wasn't waiting he was alarmed.

Had he said too much? He found Sister and asked if she had seen Petra.

'She was here, Dr Ewing. Then a Mrs Anderson arrived – Jenny's aunt. Miss Marshall left soon after that.'

'Didn't she leave any message?'

'I'm afraid not.' She looked at him curiously. 'Is anything wrong, Dr Ewing? Is there anything I can...' But he was already halfway down the corridor.

Cursing the rush hour traffic under his breath, James manipulated the car through the series of islands and one-way systems that made up the town centre. From time to time he looked at his watch. He could only guess that Petra had gone home. He visualised her making that vital telephone call – casting the die. He only hoped she was still at the same address.

At last he drew up in the quiet street outside the house where he'd dropped Petra off on the night they had dined together. He rang her bell and waited. There was no answer. Stepping back on to the pavement, he looked up. The house was in darkness. He felt his heart sink. She'd made up her mind, then. There was nothing left for him to do but go home.

Petra replaced the receiver and stood for a long time in the phone box, looking down at the silent instrument. She'd done it. She felt stunned, bemused. It had been almost uncanny – as though suddenly another being had taken her over. She could still hear her own voice, unfamiliar as a stranger's, firm and positive as she told Harry Gresham of her decision. As she stood there staring at the telephone she remembered the time when James used to ring her regularly, before they had met, when they hadn't even set eyes on each other, and her heart ached with remembered tenderness and yearning. She took a deep breath and straightened her shoulders. There was one thing left to do – and the time had come to do it.

James switched on the lights in the flat, flooding the place with light. It felt slightly less empty that way. The silence hit him like a brick wall and he switched on the stereo. The strains of the record he'd been listening to at breakfast filled the room. It was jazz, and he quickly switched it off again. It no longer matched his mood.

In the kitchen he plugged in the kettle, then unplugged it. A stiff whisky was more what he needed right now. He half filled a glass and took a deep draught, wincing a little as the fiery liquid hit the back of his throat. Then he sank into a chair, trying not to listen to the clamour inside his head. He was tired, but he'd better make himself busy tonight, he told himself grimly. The flat needed tidying. He hadn't had time to do anything this morning. Slowly he pulled himself to his feet.

He was halfway to the kitchen when his doorbell rang. He paused in the tiny hallway. One of his neighbours, no doubt. But he wasn't in a sociable mood this evening. If he was quiet perhaps whoever it was would go away – leave him to work his way out of his bleak mood. But the bell rang again, more insistently this time. James ran a hand through his hair and sighed resignedly. One of them had obviously run out of something. He'd better supply them with their half bottle of gin or cup of sugar if he wanted any peace.

The sight of her standing there, her hair damp and clinging to her cheeks and her eyes enormous with apprehension, made his heart stand still for a moment.

'Petra?'

'Yes, it's me. Can I come in?'

'Of course.' He stood aside for her to pass, closing the door after her. 'Excuse the mess.

I didn't have time...' He touched the sleeve of her coat. 'Good God, girl, you're soaking wet!'

'I know. I couldn't remember the number of the house. I left the car at the other end of the road, and even then I wasn't sure. I've been walking up and down.' They looked at each other, then she said, 'James, I've come to say that I made my decision. I rang Harry Gresham.'

'Yes?' He held his breath.

'I told him I don't want to go back to the stage. That part of my life is over. My place is here, with all my patients and – and with *you*, James.' She swallowed hard. 'I've come to say that I – want to take that next step with you. If it's not too late.'

For a long moment they looked at each other, then he took her face between his hands. 'Do you know what you're saying, Petra?'

'Yes, I know.'

'I shouldn't have handed you that ultimatum. It was thoughtless and brash of me.'

'No, you were right,' she told him. 'It was time I took charge of my life again. We can't go through life afraid of being hurt all the time. Sometimes we need to take that hundred-to-one gamble, even if it doesn't pay off.'

He smiled down at her. 'I've learned that too, since I met you.'

'We – might not be right for each other after all,' she suggested.

'Quite possible. You never know.' Now his smile teased a little.

Petra looked up at him, her mouth tremulous. 'So if you want me – here I am.'

He looked down at her. Her streaming hair and the huge appealing eyes made his heart contract. 'Do you think you could try not to look quite so sacrificial?'

'Sorry. Maybe it's the wet hair.'

'You're right.' He began to unbutton her coat. 'And you're going to catch cold if you don't get out of these wet things. I'll switch on the fire and get a towel.'

Huddled in James's dressing-gown on a cushion in front of the electric fire, Petra allowed him to towel her hair. When it was dry he turned her to him and kissed her long and deeply.

'Oh, Petra, my darling! I thought you'd never come to me,' he whispered, his lips against the tiny scar on her temple. 'I dared not let myself believe that this moment would ever come. I do love you, you know.'

'I love you too, James.' She looked up at

him. 'But that doesn't mean…'

He put a finger against her lips. 'Shh! A step at a time, remember?'

A little later he carried her into the bedroom, gently undressed her and made love to her as tenderly and sincerely as he knew how. As they lay in each other's arms afterwards, drowsily caressing, he said, 'Well, do you think you made the right decision?'

'I know I did.' Petra sighed and snuggled closer. 'I was so sure I'd worked it all out. But when I saw Jenny's happiness this evening everything just fell into place. Suddenly I knew that having someone of your own, being close to one special person, is the most precious thing there is in life. It's more important than anything else. Without that, we're nothing. To have it even for a short time is better than not at all.' She wound her arms tightly round him. 'Oh, James, I was so afraid I'd let it slip away.'

'You didn't walk up and down outside because you couldn't find the house, did you?' he asked her softly.

'No. I was plucking up my courage – terrified you might have grown tired of waiting.'

He paused, then, 'Petra, will you marry me?'

Her eyes opened wide. 'Shouldn't you

think about that first!'

He shook her gently. 'What do you imagine I've *been* thinking about these past months?'

'But you said you didn't want to be taken seriously.'

He pulled her close. 'Silly girl – that was only so as not to scare you off.'

'James,' she said solemnly, 'I know about Sarah. Val told me.'

'And *I* know about Charles what's-his-name – and what happened when you were at Maltings,' he said with a smile. 'Anna told me. So that makes us quits. But it's ancient history, Petra. What I'm interested in now is the future.' He kissed her. 'Do you think you're up to making another big decision today?'

'What if I say no?' Now it was her turn to tease. Recognising the dancing light in her eyes, he said playfully:

'Then I suppose I shall just have to set about convincing you.'

She smiled mischievously. 'In that case, Dr Ewing, I'll give you my answer tomorrow.'

347642

This Large Print Book, for people
who cannot read normal print,
is published under the auspices of

THE ULVERSCROFT FOUNDATION

... we hope you have enjoyed this book.
Please think for a moment about those
who have worse eyesight than you ...
and are unable to even read or enjoy
Large Print without great difficulty.

You can help them by sending a
donation, large or small, to:

**The Ulverscroft Foundation,
1, The Green, Bradgate Road,
Anstey, Leicestershire, LE7 7FU,
England.**
or request a copy of our brochure for
more details.

The Foundation will use all donations
to assist those people who are visually
impaired and need special attention
with medical research, diagnosis
and treatment.

Thank you very much for your help.